NICKY

Nicky Singer was born in 1956 and has worked in publishing, the arts and television. She began her writing career at the age of 15, with lyrics for a cantata *Jonah and the Whale*, and has since written four adult novels – *To Still a Child*, *To Have and to Hold*, *What She Wanted* and *Her Mother's Daughter* – and two works of non-fiction – *The Tiny Book of Time* (with Kim Pickin) and *The Little Book of the Millennium* (with Jackie Singer). Her first children's book, *Feather Boy*, won the Blue Peter Children's Book Award and has sold in eighteen countries. She was co-founder and co-director (1987-1996) of Performing Arts Labs, a charity dedicated to training new writers for theatre, screen and opera. In 1995 she presented BBC2's highly acclaimed documentary series on women's fertility, *Labours of Eve*, and wrote the preface to the book which accompanied the series. Nicky Singer lives in Brighton with her husband, their two sons and a daughter.

ACKNOWLEDGEMENTS

Many people helped make this book. I particularly thank those brave enough to share personal or family stories of alcoholism and self-harm: notably Justina, Lea, Deano, and my own sister, Jane. Dr Hugh Williams was a generous and informative guide on the Substance Misuse Service (any errors are mine) and I'm particularly grateful to the patients of the Westbourne Hospital for their honesty and their trust.

I pay tribute to all those who spoke to me of adoption, especially Vanessa Gebby, Alex Boyd and my dreamer of dreams, Tom Russell. I learned from all of them.

I'm grateful to Gary Stewart, who knows more about markets than most, and to Richard Curd who allowed me to prowl round his excellent Brighton restaurant Richard's Brasserie. Any dried sea-sponges or blood-letting are entirely my own invention.

I thank teenagers Charlotte Goodman and Laura Hopkins: Charlotte for advice on teenage girls and Laura for reading the manuscript for neanderthal expressions.

I thank, as always, my agent Clare Conville, who makes my life happy.

Lastly I send a big hug to Gillie Russell, Publishing Director at HarperCollins. She knows what she did. Thank you, Gillie.

NICKY SINGER

doll

An imprint of HarperCollins*Publishers*

By the same author
Feather Boy

First published in Great Britain by CollinsFlamingo 2003

1 3 5 7 9 8 6 4 2

CollinsFlamingo is an imprint of HarperCollins*Publishers* Ltd,
77-85 Fulham Palace Road, Hammersmith, London W6 8JB

The HarperCollins website address is www.**fire**and**water**.com

ISBN 0 00 715416 X

Printed and bound in Great Britain by Clays Ltd, St Ives plc

For Tom
who also speaks to stars

The night my mother died she gave me a doll.

"This is for you, beloved," she whispered, her voice soft and low. "Hold it next to your heart. And I will be with you. Always."

And of course I didn't look at the doll then, because I was looking at my mother. Her big, beautiful, belligerent body calm at last. Hushed on the bed. Her black hair pushed away from her face. Her eyes – ever that startling blue – placid now. Her skin pale, the waxy cream of the candles I lit around her, church candles, fifteen of them. Her choice, as were the roses I'd gathered in armfuls from the garden.

"Let them be red," my mother said.

And they were red. Petals the colour of blood.

She smiled then. Despite everything she smiled.

"Light the incense," she smiled.

And I did. Cinnamon. Which is for healing but also for love.

"Healing!" my grandmother exclaimed.

And I might have riposted "Love!" But I didn't. I just sat beside my mother and held her hand until I heard her breathe out but not breathe in again. There was a pause in which a clock ticked. Tick. Tick. Then my grandmother came to the bedside, slid my mother's eyelids shut and everything went dark.

"Let go now, Tilly," grandmother said.

And when I didn't let go, she leaned down and took our clasped hands (my mother's and mine, her daughter's and her granddaughter's) and prised our fingers apart. She was not ungentle. And I was glad in a way, because I cannot see otherwise how I could have released my mother's hand. I would have had to stay sitting there for ever.

"Go to your room," Grandma said. "I'll deal with everything here."

And I went. Gratefully. The smell of cinnamon still on me.

It might be five minutes since I left my mother's room. It might be five hours. I have lost track of time. These things only I know: my grandmother is not in the house; the night is still dark; I'm out on the swing.

My father put up this swing. Screwed rings into the outstretched limb of a tree and hung the chains. The rings used to be greased but now they're dry and rusty. They squeak. A rhythmic squeak, in time with my swing. My bare arms are around the chains, like I am hugging them. The metal is cold and so is the night wind. All the hairs on my forearms are standing up in protest. But I don't care about the cold. In fact I'm glad of the cold. It makes me feel alive. Under my feet the ground is wet. When I was six I wore this patch to mud. I came to swing and swing and tell myself stories. All the stories had happy endings.

"You're not a child any more," says Grandma.

And I'm not. I'm fourteen years old. But there's mud beneath the swing once more. I've started to come here again. To tell stories – maybe, but also to think. Tonight, I've come to look at the doll.

It's a small thing, no bigger than my hand, and

quite unlike the thousand other dolls my mother made. This doll is not sewn of remnants and jumble fabrics. It's made out of material my mother wore next to her own skin. Her face (for the doll is a girl, a woman), her hands, her feet, in fact all of her flesh is cut from my mother's white kid gloves. The long ones. The ones that went to her elbows.

"Every woman," said my mother, "should have a pair of white kid gloves, at least once in her lifetime."

I touch the doll's face, run a thumb across her tiny cheek. The flesh is warm, supple, animal. Then I can't help lifting the doll to my face. And there she is, my mother, the conflicting scents of her: jasmine, leather, sweat, candle wax, engine oil. And, and... that thin, distilled, sweet odour that makes my heart reel.

"*I don't know what you're talking about, Tilly,*" says my grandmother.

I swing harder, higher. The chain creaks, a soothing rhythmic creak. The wind blusters against my face. I'm cold. I'm alive. My mother loved me, loves me, gave me this doll.

I lift the doll again, look again. The dolls my mother made to sell wore dresses. This one wears trousers. Black leather trousers. And I know at once what the leather has been cut from. My mother's biking gear. And now I am a child again. Five years old, waiting at the playground. Last to be collected – as usual – the teacher tutting, clicking her fingers. Then a roar from around the corner, the screech of brakes, and a huge figure dressed head to toe in black advancing towards the child and the clicking teacher.

"Has your mother got a bike now?" asks Miss Pretty.

I shake my head. Because my mother doesn't have a bike. At least she didn't when I left home that morning. Besides, this huge advancing thing cannot be my mother. Its head is too big. The figure stops. It takes off its hat.

"Surprise!" it says and peals laughter.

She swings my schoolbag round her neck, and puts me astride the bike. The saddle is wider than my splayed legs, or so it seems to me.

"Hold on," my mother cries and puts the hat over my head. It's heavy and it doesn't fit, even with the strap pulled to its tightest. I can't breathe.

My mother gets on in front of me.

"Hold on," she shouts and revs the engine. Hold on to what: the hat, the bike, my mother's too-big waist? I glance imploringly at Miss Pretty and then we are off. Instinct alone preserves me. I dig my nails into the ridged hem of the leather jacket, I clutch and clutch. The hat bounces and throttles.

"Isn't it wonderful?" My mother's voice comes by on the wind.

"Didn't you love it?" she says when we stop.

"Yes," I say. "Yes. I loved it."

Later, when my father finds out, he shouts at her. The first of the rows I actually remember.

"I gave her the helmet," my mother cries indignantly. "What's the fuss? Anyway, she loved it. She said so. Didn't you, Tilly?"

Later my mother took me aside. "Pay attention, Tilly," she said. "A bike's not a method of transport. A bike's freedom."

And it is to these bike leathers my mother took her scissors. I imagine that first impossible cut. My mother knifing through – what? The jacket? The trousers? The trousers probably. The leather thinner there. I can hear the sound, that slight crunch as the metal blades close on skin. Animal skin. And human skin. For that's what cutting the leathers would have felt like to my mother. Like cutting her own skin. Yet she did it. For the doll.

For me.

What else has she cut? The doll's bodice is velvet, a strokable patchwork of my mother's more sumptuous tastes. A fragment of magenta, from a scarf probably. A snippet of gold, the trimming of that black evening gown, and yes, a tiny scrap of white from her "purity jacket".

"For atonement," she said, kissing me and going out with my father in the days when they still did such things. I was four, I think, I didn't know what "atonement" meant. Though it meant, for a while, that my mother stayed closer by me.

I move on to the doll's face. The hair is jet black and straight. You buy it in curls, so my mother must have brushed and brushed it to be like this. She has also shaped a fringe.

"Don't you think you're too old to have a fringe now, Judith?" Grandma asked her.

"No," said my mother.

The doll's eyes are blue. Two startling June-sky sequins with a sewn black centre. And the mouth is smiling.

But what's this? This thing around the doll's left wrist? A bracelet of tiny red glass beads, wound tight so they cut into the flesh a little. What can this mean? My mother never had anything so flimsy. She wore bone and amber and circlets of silver. And she never wore red, except on her lips. The bracelet is an impostor, I feel like ripping it off, freeing that left wrist. But this is my mother's gift to me.

Swing, Tilly, swing.

"Tilly? Tilly!" It is my grandmother. She has returned. She knows where to find me.

"Come in, Tilly," she says. "Please."

I slow the swing, put my feet to the mud, slip the doll into my pocket. For the doll is just between me and my mother.

"You must be chilled to the bone," says Grandma.

"I'm alive," I say.

"Oh, Tilly." She takes my hand and leads me inside. I am content to be led. Now that she is holding me I feel a rush of exhaustion. I want to lie down. I want to be asleep. Although I do not expect to sleep. Not for a long time.

She brings me to my room. Rubs and rubs my hand, as if to find blood. Then she goes to my bed and unfolds my nightdress.

"I'll be OK."

"Sure?" she asks.

"Yes."

She bends to kiss me. When my grandmother was a child her father pressed a black cane against her spine to teach her the virtue of a straight back. She bends like the rod is still there. Sometimes I think there will be one kiss too many and then she'll snap in two.

"Goodnight," she says, though it cannot be a good night.

I wait till she closes the door and then I slip, naked, into bed. The doll is still in my hand. Have I been delaying this moment? No longer. I press the doll against my heart. For a moment there's nothing. Nothing at all. All my expectations roar with panic. For there has to be something, something I can feel, something I can know, trust. And then it comes, a warmth, a small fire just beneath my hands. And of course it could just be my hands, the rubbed blood clasp of them, but I don't think so. I think it's the doll.

My mother wired her dolls so they could bend, move. I watched her do it so many times. This doll has a wired spine and wired limbs. I'm not pressing now, more pulling, pulling the doll into my heart and I can feel that spine and those wires and, somewhere deeper still, the fevered thud of life. And yes, maybe it's just my life. My heart beating. But it comforts me. So I don't move the doll and I don't move my hands.

I'm still lying like this when I hear the door open again. It's Grandma. She's checking to see if I am asleep. I keep quite still and she doesn't come any closer, just quietly shuts the door. The pretence suits both of us. We have lived a long time together, my grandmother and I.

Later, I know I have slept because I wake again. And there's a moment in that waking when I hope, I dream, that everything that has happened, has not happened. Then I see the doll. It's moved in the night. It lies on my pillow and its face is wet. And I have this lurching idea that the doll has been crying. But maybe it was only me crying. I scoop up the doll, hold it. Hold her.

Then I listen.

Downstairs there is noise. Grandma, who has never slept well, is up already. I hear the clatter of her in the kitchen. She will have laid a table, put out napkins. What else will she have done?

I rise silently and get dressed for school. We all

need things to be ordinary. This is the game Grandma and I play. I tuck the doll into my skirt pocket and move with agile silence along the corridor to my mother's room. The door is ajar.

And of course, I do not want to enter there. I do not want to see again anything that I have seen.

"What are you then?" my mother says. *"A mouse?"*

So I go in.

The room is tidy and the bed made, which alone proves that my mother is dead. For if my mother lived there would be mess everywhere. Drawers agape, clothes on the floor, lids off lipstick. But there is no mess. There are no candles. No cinnamon sticks. Even the flowers are gone. The window is wide open and the morning air abrasively clean. In the night, Grandma has scrubbed the carpet. Got down on her stiff knees with the disinfectant. If there were stains – if there were spots – on that carpet last night, there won't be now. But there were no spots. There were just rose petals, red rose petals. That was all. I was there. It was a good death, the death she would have wanted.

"Always tell the truth, Tilly," says my mother. *"The truth is important. Yes?"*

"Tilly." It's Grandma calling. "Is that you?" I move quickly into the corridor, pretend that I've just come from the bathroom.

"Oh, good, you're up. Breakfast's made."

The smell of bacon fat curls up the stairs. I go down to the kitchen. Grandma is also frying sausages, tomatoes, mushrooms. As I come in she cracks two eggs.

"You know I don't eat breakfast."

"Well, you should. You must. Breakfast sets you up for the day."

We have had this discussion a thousand times. I don't want to have it this morning. I make for the fridge, for juice. Then I see the breakfast table. It's laid for three.

I round on her. "You've told him, haven't you? You called him."

"Of course," my grandmother says. "What did you expect?" And then: "He's family."

As if in confirmation of this fact, the doorbell rings.

I watch her unyielding walk to the porch.

"Margaret." My father steps into the hall, greets my grandmother and then turns immediately to me. "Tilly, I'm so sorry."

He walks straight down the corridor and, uninvited, puts his arms around me. As I stand like a stone in his embrace, I think: this is what it must be like to be hugged by a stranger. Although he's not a stranger. I see him most weekends.

Then he says something else. He says: "Grandma told me. Grandma says it was you who found her."

And I feel a pricking hotness in my face, as though he'd accused me of lying. And something in me wants to shout, but I put my hand on the doll and keep my mouth clamped shut.

He releases me. He's a small man. Small and mobile and the colour of sand. How could my huge, dark mother have loved him?

"Tilly..." he begins.

"Don't worry, Richard," says Grandma. "I'm here. I'll be here. I'll look after her. We'll be fine, won't we Tilly?"

"Yes," I say then.

He looks relieved.

"There's coffee, Richard," says Grandma. "And breakfast if you haven't eaten."

"Of course he hasn't eaten," I say. "He eats at the restaurant. That's why he's always gone so early." I say it on autopilot, like my mother used to say it, half bitterly, half to explain why he was never here of a morning.

My father looks at his watch.

"I expect you're busy," I mimic. "I expect you've got a lot on."

"Tilly..." warns Grandma.

"It's OK," says my father. "It's the shock."

"Hardly a shock," says Grandma.

My father sits down. My mother's mother brings him coffee, serves him a man's breakfast. The plate steams.

"How can you eat?" I say.

"Everyone has to eat," says Grandma.

"I'll let the school know," says my father. "I'll drive you in, Tilly. Speak to the Head."

"No!"

It sounds like a gasp. Grandma looks at me, moves to my side, takes my hand.

"No need, Richard," she says smoothly. "I'll deal with all that."

"But—" he protests.

"It's fine, Richard. It'll be fine. You have enough to do."

"Enough" means work. Grandma likes a man to work. Her husband always worked, Gerry. Worked long hours, worked long distances, was a travelling salesman. Good commission, until he ran his car into a tree. Still got Salesman of the Week though, even though he died on the Thursday. Had more Tupperware receipts in his pocket that day than most salesmen got in a month. That's what was said, proudly, at his funeral. His daughter, my mother, was fourteen at the time. The same age I am now.

"Well," says my father, "if you're sure."

"I'm sure," she says.

He looks uncomfortable. Says to me, knife poised, "Aren't you having any?"

"I'm not hungry." He should put down that knife. The light on the blade is bouncing in my eyes.

"She's a stick. A rake. How can she be the daughter of a restaurateur and be so uninterested in food? You should feed her up, Richard."

"She knows she's welcome in the restaurant any time." He looks up at me, blade still upright. "In fact, you can come back with me, Tilly. Stay until – well, you know."

"Put down the knife," I say.

"What?"

"The knife. Put it down!"

Grandma moves swiftly, pushes my father's knife into his bacon, as though he were a child.

"What—"

Then she backs off, stands against the counter. "Sorry, Richard," she says and half nods at me. Adding quickly, "And don't worry about the arrangements. I'll take care of everything."

And I know why she's standing there.

My father re-groups. "I don't know what we'd all do without you, Margaret," he says.

She's standing there because of the Sabatier block.

I edge towards the counter myself, but I keep my eyes on my father.

"You'll let me know – what happens?" he says.

"Of course," says Grandma.

"We'll need to talk about a long-term solution. Tilly can't stay here, not now, not after..."

I expect to see a gap. One knife missing. The long, thin-bladed carving knife. But, as I turn and glance, I see it. The knife. Washed and dried and in its place. Grandma. Oh Grandma.

"No need to rush into things," says Grandma. "Take one day at a time. That's the best way."

My father drains his coffee. "You don't have to go to school, Tilly," he says. "I'm sure they'd understand."

"Best to keep busy," says Grandma. "What would she do here, anyway?"

"Tilly?"

"I want to go." It's a kind of whisper.

"OK. Your choice." He pauses. "Do you still want to come to the restaurant on Sunday?"

"Of course she does," says Grandma.

"Tilly?"

"If you want."

"Well, I am short-staffed. It would help."

"OK then."

"Thanks, Tilly." He stands up. He comes for a kiss, or a touch, but I move away and his arms fall short. "Just one thing," he says. "It's not your fault. You do understand that, don't you Tilly? Nothing that's happened is your fault."

Why does he have to say these things?

"Of course she understands that," says Grandma. "Now come on, Tilly. We have to go."

She puts her body between my father's and mine, directs him towards the door.

"Goodbye then," he says.

I watch my father drive away. What strikes me most about him this morning is that he is alive. And that doesn't seem fair somehow.

The drive to the school gates is fifteen minutes, but

Grandma doesn't take me to the gates. She pulls the car up four roads short. Looks in all her mirrors.

"OK?" she says.

"Yes. Thanks Grandma."

I also check the road. Sometimes Mercy's friend Charlie walks this way. But more often she gets the bus and the bus doesn't come down this street. I can see no one but a man and his dog. I give my Grandma a peck on her dry cheek.

"It'll be all right," says Grandma. "Don't worry about a thing. Promise me?"

I get out and watch while Grandma turns the car and drives away. Until this moment, I have no doubt that I'm going to school. It's not as if I don't know the way. I've walked the route from here more times than I care to remember. But, as my grandmother's car disappears from view, so does my certainty. It's as though, by turning the corner, she has cut me adrift. School doesn't seem the point any more. Even the word "school" seems to have shifted. I can't fix on its meaning. I stand bewildered. I seem not to know what to do or where to go.

And then I hear a voice, soft and low. "I know," the voice says. And then it whispers: "Come."

2

"Jan, Jan – do you hear me, Jan?"

He does hear her, though he does not reply. He listens to the soft way she articulates the first letter of his name, making the J into a Y: *Yan, Yan*. There is a yearning in that letter, a yearning in the way she calls, he thinks, even now. But he shuts it out, shuts her out. Not that he does not love his mother, his English mother. He does.

He is simply not in the room. Which is to say, his body may be sitting on the bed, his shoes scuffing the floor, but his mind is up at the railway track. He goes there often, both in his head and on foot. There is something in the wind up there, the noise it makes as it crosses the desolate bridge. A high, melancholy, mountain sound. A sound he thinks he recognises, though of course he cannot recognise it, for it is only wind over a bridge. But he goes there to check. This morning he took his pipes. The Antara, panpipes from Bolivia. The strong reeds bound together with wood and string and brightly coloured wool. He hid them under his shirt. Though there is no one up at the bridge to look. Usually.

Why did he go today? He never goes during school. School is important, he knows that. Was it the bridge, the music, calling him? Or was it that moment when his mother said, as he stood in the hall checking his books: "I think it's going to be cold. You should take a coat."? As though he was five not fifteen. Is that why he walked out of the door and turned left, not right? Life pivots, Jan thinks, on such tiny decisions. The moment when you elect, for whatever reason, to choose this road rather than that. Other people might call it chance, or coincidence. But Jan has a sense of a purposeful universe. The railway line has been waiting.

And so he climbs, without any hurry, street after street, towards the edge of the town and the opening, which runs by the graveyard of St Thomas, out to the field and the railway beyond. It is not a place that invites company. There is no path, except the one that Jan has trod, and the wilderness covers what tracks he makes soon enough. The nettles grow high and undisturbed and, where the mound of the railway begins to rise, brambles stretch like lashes. Jan takes a stick and beats them back, like a latter-day prince clearing a way to a castle. And, today, there is a princess.

Or at least a figure. Standing right at the edge of the bridge. His bridge. He is so astonished he almost drops the pipes, but they are suspended around his neck on a black plait of Bolivian wool. Perhaps he has imagined the figure? He does imagine things. He's aware of that. But this figure moves; it swings around to look down the track. A girl. He knows, at once, what she's doing. She's trying to guess when the next train will come.

He knows this because he has stood where she stands now. The bridge is over a river. It's narrow. Four tracks pass here. There is very little space between the outer tracks and the low wall of the bridge. If you were to run alongside the wall when a train was passing, and they pass at over a hundred miles an hour, you would not, Jan thinks, survive. Unless that is, the train was using one of the centre tracks, and you couldn't know that until the engine was almost upon you. And even then the wind might knock you to the ground. Jan has listened to this wind too. The displaced air of a train coming. It whines like a circular saw. Unless it's one of the twelve-coach passenger trains, which has a softer, plusher sound.

The girl is already too close. She is almost on the bridge. She's a small thing, slight, with cropped dark hair. One would barely have to puff, he thinks, to blow her over. He could almost do it from where he's standing, in the lee of the elderflower tree, twenty metres away.

Her head is averted now. He cannot see her face, but he knows she's calculating. *Can I do it? Can I cross the bridge in safety?* The thoughts he thought, when he also stood there, poised. Only he walked away. You'd have to be prepared to die to run by the wall. You'd have not to mind which way it fell out. Left or right. And he'd wanted to live.

You see, he has already died once. When he was a baby. His was a difficult birth in a difficult country. Chile. They looked at the scrap of him and put him on a life-support machine. An hour later someone decided to blow up one of Pinochet's power stations. The cot died then, but the scrap of life didn't. It breathed for itself until the spare generator kicked in.

You might not be lucky twice, Jan thinks. Which is why he doesn't run the bridge.

There's a low rumble further down the track. Jan listens, quick and intent. It is, he thinks, the sound of the train that forks off before it gets to this bridge, about half a mile away. He recognises the drone. But the girl can't know that. She'll wait for it to pass, thinking, as he did once, that if you wait for a train, there can't be another one immediately. So you'll be safe. You'll have the two or three minutes you need. That's a fine calculation in itself – how many minutes will it take you to run the seventy-metre bridge? If a world-class athlete can do a hundred metres in under ten seconds then...

She's running. He cannot believe his eyes; the girl is running. What if he's wrong about the train and the fork? What if the train is coming right here, right now? A sound explodes out of his mouth. He thinks it's "Stop!" But it would be madness to stop now, she must keep going, she must run faster than she's ever run in her life, just in case. He can still hear the rumble, it's gone on too long, the train must be past the fork and the girl is still running, running like in a dream where no matter how fast you run, you never move forward at all.

And then – she's arrived. She's at the other side. And there is no train. No rumble even. The train has gone the other way.

She's a good distance from him now, a dark silhouette against the sky, and yet he feels her flash of triumph, sees it in the defiant stamp of her body. *Yes, I did it. I ran the bridge.* Then her head drops, she's holding something. It's a doll. A small doll, no bigger than her hand. How can he know that when he's so far away? And yet he does know.

Jan leans from his bed, in the bedroom of his very English house, and opens a drawer. He extracts a tiny painted box, lifts the lid. There are seven Worry People in this box: three men, three women, one child. They are made of matchwood, their bodies bound with brightly coloured cotton and vibrant scraps of cloth: blue, purple, pink, red. All except one, and it is this doll – Violeta – that Jan lifts out and puts in the palm of his hand. This doll is made of wire, the cotton bindings a dull yellow, the skirt the colour of baked mud. Its face is orange paper and, though it has black eyes and a black nose, it has no mouth. Its hair is black and sparkling, as though it were made of sand and tarmac. Its wire arms are uneven, one outstretched towards him, the other a rusted stub. The doll is only half a thumb high. He closes his hand around it. Oh yes, he knows. He holds the doll for a moment, then puts it back in the box with the others and returns the box to his bedside drawer.

In the eye of his mind, he watches the way the girl touches her doll, observes again how she closes the doll against her chest. That's when she realises, he thinks. She has to run again. There is no way back, unless she wants to swim the river.

She begins at once. Her hand still on her heart. Starts to cross for a second time. But she isn't running now, she's jogging. Barely that, she's ambling. It's the confidence; she doesn't have to hurry. The doll has absorbed her fear. Is that why she doesn't react to the noise down the track? It's loud enough. Not a drone this time but the circular-saw noise. Surely she can hear it? The whine of the Intercity. The whoosh of pushed air and, coming closer, the scream of speeding metal? There is no alarm at all on her face. And she's looking right at him now, gliding across the bridge towards the oncoming train. Her face a moon of content. He wants to go on to the bridge and shake her. Hurry her up.

Time is passing so slowly and still the train comes. She must be able to see it now, though he has his back to it. Hurry up. Run. Run! The train is not air now but thundering steel, bawling and sparking down the track. And then it's past him and she's still on the bridge. Against the wall on the inside track, where the train is coming. There's a moment, a long, eight-coach moment, when he can see nothing but moving metal. And then, like an arrow, the train's gone.

But the girl remains. She's at the edge of the bridge. Bending down, picking a flower. And now he really does want to shake her. Now he wants to pick her up and punch her in the face, even though she's small and he doesn't know her. How dare she! How could she put him through that! He moves out from the shadow of the elderflower tree (although he's not given to interventions) and walks towards her. She stands up. But not, he thinks, because she hears him, but because she's finished looking at the flower. Her skin is creamy pale though there's a flush in her cheeks, he notices as he comes closer, and her eyes, which are so dark they look almost black, have a wild brightness in them.

For a moment she doesn't seem to register him. And then, quick and defensive, she moves her body square to his, glares up at him. And something in him wants to laugh, she looks so ridiculous, a fierce little sprite who's nevertheless run the bridge. But he doesn't laugh, partly because of the intensity of her gaze, which makes him feel the intruder, and partly because of the doll. Around its neck are large ungainly stitches, black, like you use to sew up a wound.

She feels his eyes, snatches the doll from his sight.

"What's it to you?" she yells, the spots in her cheeks burning.

And then she's off, tumbling down the mound, flailing through the brambled undergrowth, and on, into the field beyond. As though he's after her. Which, of course, he is not.

He watches her for as long as she stays in view. Her body fighting, jagged and twisting, even when the terrain gets easier. He is ashamed to have sent her on this desperate flight.

But he knows what he saw.

"Jan, Jan." His mother is coming. Her footfalls are on the stairs.

But he certainly cannot answer his mother now. He must reach the end of his thought. He needs to say aloud the thing that he has not been saying aloud. The thing that is worrying him although, as the girl said, it's nothing to do with him. But it is to do with him. Why else would the blood beat so hard in his breast?

"Jan!" His mother comes into the room. "Didn't you hear me?"

He heard her.

"Jan, oh Jan." She sits down beside him on the bed. "Jan, they rang me at work. They said you didn't go in today. Why is that, Jan?"

He doesn't know. He knows only he had to be at the bridge.

"You understand how important your education is, don't you, Jan? You can do nothing, be nothing, without it. Tell me you understand?"

He understands.

"Jan, why don't you speak to me?"

Jan has nothing to say on the subject of education.

"Jan, please speak to me."

"The doll," Jan says aloud, "I think it's evil."

3

Gerda.

This is the name of the doll. It came to me on the bridge, when I was running. Running like I was the wind and the trains were paper.

"Trust me. Trust me, trust me, trust me." The noise of the wind and the wheels and the wings at my feet. Did she whisper the name to me herself? Or was it my mother's voice I heard? I don't know. But the name is right. The name of the child in the Snow Queen. How I loved that story. Had my mother read it over and over again. In those long-ago, happy-ever-after days. How the little girl scoured the world for Kai, the boy with ice in his heart, and how she found him, and held him, and how her tears melted that ice.

And I do trust Gerda. Know that I would follow her to the ends of the earth. Knew it from the moment she uttered that first word: "Come." Was I waiting for her to speak? It didn't surprise me. I've always believed that love can stretch between worlds. That the dead can speak. That the past stands close enough to whisper in your ear.

"We're Weavers," said my mother. "Judith and Tilly Weaver. Weaver by name and weaver by nature. Matilda Weaver. It's your name but also who and what you are. We Weavers are the weft and the warp, we web things together."

My father argued with her about that. "You're only a Weaver by marriage," he said. "You were born a Barker." That's how he crushed her. With small things.

"A name isn't a small thing," said Inti. Inti was the molten-eyed Ecuadorian who had the stall next to my mother at the market. "There's one tribe," he said, "that never reveal their names to strangers. They believe if a stranger knows your name, he can tramp on your soul."

And so the day passes in thinking, wandering, wondering, being close. I am content, happy even. I remember how, when I was a small child, I was afraid of the dark. Each night, in order to sleep, I constructed in my imagination fifteen concentric courtyards, each with high stone walls and only one door. And then I walked myself through each one of those doors, locking it behind me. In the innermost courtyard, the fifteenth, was a small square of grass. I bolted the final door, lay down on the grass and slept. Gerda makes me feel as I did in that courtyard. Safe.

So it is a shock to find myself, at dusk, at the glass entrance of the shopping mall. How did we arrive here? Why have we stopped? This is not my place. It belongs to those who thrive in artificial light. It is Mercy's place. Charlie's place.

And there they are, the electronic doors swishing open for them. They are coming towards me. Mercedes Van Day and Charlotte Ferguson. Mercy half a step in front. She is captivatingly beautiful. I thought so when she was my friend and I still think so. She's one of those people from whom you cannot take your eyes. Her skin is flawless, translucent even, as if, beneath the surface, where others have boiling pimples, she has radiant light. I've never seen such skin, even on an adult. Her blonde hair swings, impeccably cut, about her face and her eyes are like a cat's, at once quick and stealthy. They promise you things. Her body is both slim and curved and she has that ability to turn a collar, or hitch a hem so that she looks stylish, individual even in her school uniform. Charlie is larger and darker and drawn to Mercy, as I was, like a moth to a flame.

There is a spring in Mercy's step. She has made a new purchase. At her side is one of those shining paper carriers with the string handles they give you in designer shops. She will have gone with Charlie for a post-school coffee, and been unable to resist – what? A belt? A skimpy top? A pair of shoes? She smiles and talks and walks towards me.

I've tried to walk like that, so the sea of people in front of you parts when you move. I've tried to cut my hair so it falls, as hers does, like a kiss against her cheek.

"You are who you are," said my mother, one foot on the accelerator of her Yamaha Virago 750. "Why try to be someone else?"

"Be yourself," my mother said, providing me with a non-regulation school jumper. "Why not?"

And of course, I've wanted to be as fearless as my mother, as devil-may-care, but not as much as I've wanted to be Mercedes Van Day.

They are almost upon me, Mercy and Charlie, but their heads are so close in conversation, they will not see me. I have time to melt away. I choose the bus shelter. I need to be calm, to compose my thinking.

"Inti," says Gerda. "Concentrate on Inti."

Inti, my mother's friend, the gap-toothed South American. Inti, the market man who sold amber and lapis lazuli and opals.

Mercy and Charlie are coming towards the bus stop.

And also panpipes. Inti, who took me on his lap when my mother was busy and told me the names of the Siku, the Latin pipes. Whispered Antara and Malta. Showed me how to fill the bamboo reeds with tiny green seeds. "You have to tune pipes," Inti said, "in winter. When the pipes are cold, they play too low."

Mercy and Charlie are going home. They are going by bus. They are taking the bus from this stop.

"*Taquiri de Jaine*," says Gerda.

The rhythm of the carnival, Inti's favourite tune. I try to listen to it. But all I hear is the flip of two plastic seats. Mercy and Charlie sit down. And there I am, in the corner, trapped.

Mercy and Charlie are animated, they talk loudly, excitedly. They are discussing "Celeb Night". It's a charity affair, in aid of the NSPCC, and Mercy's mother is one of the organisers. Come dressed as your favourite star, that was the original idea. It was Mrs Van Day who introduced the idea of a talent contest. "Like they do on the television. Aspiring bands. Singers. A pound if you want to cast a vote."

Everyone's going. Mrs Van Day's promised the press, scouts from the music business. Everyone that is, except me. Why would I want to?

Mercy is going as Britney Spears. She has the body, the smile, the eyes and she's bought the hair extensions. Now all she needs is a dress.

"Well, actually," she's telling Charlie, "I'm going to have trousers and a top. Cindy, you know my mother's friend Cindy? The dressmaker?"

"Your mother!" exclaims Charlie. "If she wanted a photographer from *Hello!* she'd have one for a friend."

"Yeah, well. Cindy's copying something from a magazine. Something Britney actually wore. It's gauze mostly. Blue gauze. It's going to be amazing. Just you wait. Got a fitting on Sunday. Got to look my best, you see." Mercy pauses. "Jan's coming."

"Jan?" queries Charlie.

"Yes. It's spelt with a J but pronounced like a Y. Yan.

Yan Spark. And that's his real name, not a stage name. How cool is that? Ready-made star quality. But he's the strong silent type, you see. So I'm going to need more than my sparkling conversation."

"Is he going in for the contest?"

"Of course. He's Mr Guitar, apparently. Plays brilliantly, according to his mother who told my mother. But forget guitar, you should take a look at his face. Is he gorgeous or what? His features, Charlie, they're kind of sculpted. Like he was some Inca god. And his eyes, they're so dark, so deep you feel like you are looking down a tunnel right into his soul. And..."

And then, with her boy, comes my boy. The one up at the bridge. I've felt him tracking me all day, a hound at my back. But I haven't turned round once to look. Because of his eyes. They are not tunnels you can look down, they are fierce, dark drills. They bore into you. Make you feel that, with a glance, he could pierce your heart right through. Know things about you that even you don't know.

But I could have stood that. Wouldn't have cared, except that, at the bridge, he turned those eyes on Gerda. Stared like he could see right through her, too.

My Gerda. And I couldn't bear that again. Stared and stared, as if he had the right. As if he knew something.

I cannot stop my hand, it's reaching into my pocket. I have to touch her. Put my fingers on Gerda's warm, white skin. My breath is slamming against the glass of the bus shelter.

This is for you, beloved.

But somehow I fumble. A bus is coming and someone is barging and pushing. It's an old lady and the handle of her shopping bag is snagged round my arm. I cry out, so as not to drop Gerda. The old woman pulls against me, glares, curses and butts her way on to the bus. I'm still spinning when Mercy says:

"Well, well. If it isn't Tilly M."

I come to a stop. We are face to face. Mercy is not getting on the bus. Not this bus anyway.

"Did you bunk off school today to assault senior citizens?"

Charlie sniggers.

I work at composing my features, pay attention to keeping my hand so still she will not see what is clutched at my heart.

"What's that then?" she asks.

Did I look at Gerda? Did I?

"It's one of those creepy things her mum makes," Charlie says.

"Oh," says Mercy. "A little dolly. Let's see then."

A second bus arrives. This has to be their bus. People shuffle and move. Mercy and Charlie don't move. They stay. The bus drives away. I could run. I could run again. If Mercy touches the doll... If she brings her hand anywhere near...

"I said, let's see."

"No!" I jam Gerda into my pocket. And then: "Nothing to see."

"How old are you, Tilly?" Mercy laughs. And I remember how that laugh used to be full of kindness. How it seemed "quaint" to her that I came to school dressed in non-regulation cardigans and black gym shoes when everyone else had trainers. Mercy was so sure of herself that difference didn't seem to matter. How I adored her for that. And how bereft I was the day it stopped. The day she came to my house.

"I said, how old are you, Make-Believe?"

Make-Believe. That was my fault too, of course. I wouldn't tell them my middle name. Mercedes Alice Van Day. Charlotte Elizabeth Ferguson. Matilda M. Weaver. They all had middle names but I didn't, or not one I was prepared to admit to. Was I afraid they would trample my soul? No. I never shared the secret with Mercy, not even when we were at our closest. The reason was – shame. And, give credit where credit's due, Mercy never pushed me. Other people did. Small enquiries, a few tentative jokes. But I never cared. What were a few jokes compared with the truth?

It was Charlie who wouldn't let go. It was how she wormed into Mercy's affection. How she pushed me away.

"What does the M stand for, Weaver? Go on, tell us. What's the big deal? Friends are meant to share. Anyway, it's only a game."

A Rumpelstiltskin game. What is Tilly's middle name? Guess, guess, have a good laugh. Tilly Moron, Tilly Misbegotten, Tilly Misery-Guts, Tilly Misfit, Tilly Misnomer and then Tilly Make-Believe.

It was Mercy who coined it.

"Make-Believe," she said, "it's Make-Believe, isn't it?"

And I said yes. To stop the game, but also because it didn't seem that unkind. There was something innocent in it, something creative, it contained the dust of fairies and of angels. And of course, after that day at my mother's house, she'd called me many worse things, bitter things. So "Make-Believe" sounded, in my ears, like reconciliation. And I wanted her friendship so much. I wanted her back. How she was, how it all was, before...

"I'm waiting," says Mercy and she stands, her bus seat twanging upright behind her.

Nothing can happen. This is a bus shelter. A shelter. There are other people here. A second old lady, looking the other way. A mother, fussing over a toddler. Or maybe the toddler's fussing.

"Are you deaf? As well as infantile? Bet you still have Barbies too."

"Walk away," says Gerda.

"I saw you this morning," Charlie says then. "In Tisbury Road."

But she can't have. I looked up and down the street. I looked for her bus.

"That's where your grandma drops you, when your mum—"

Mum. Not even I called my mother "Mum". I called her "Mama" because this – along with Weaver – is what she called herself. My father called her "Judith". Inti called her "Big". No, I will not have my mother in Charlie's mouth.

"Leave my mother out of this," I shout.

"Whoa," says Mercy. "Steady on."

"As I was saying," says Charlie, "your grandma drops you in Tisbury Road when your mother—"

"Shut your mouth. Shut it!" The second old lady tuts and turns to the mother with the toddler. The toddler bursts into tears.

"You're upsetting the baby now," says Mercy.

I will not cry.

I will not be angry.

"Mustn't lose your temper," says my grandmother. "You have a terrible temper, Tilly. How would it be if we all allowed ourselves to lose our tempers? Self-control. That's something I learnt from Gerry. My husband never lost his temper."

"Your mother—" says Charlie.

"Walk away," says Gerda.

"My mother," I scream, "is dead. Dead. Dead. Dead!"

"Oh sure," says Mercy. And she laughs.

4

Jan is dreaming. In the dream he takes the pipes and he can play. Runs his lips along the bamboo openings, and breathes into the hollow canes. The sound that returns to him is the one he recognises; the sound of mountains and wind and his own soul. A love song and yet one of longing. His body echoes with it, as if the instrument was his own hollowed bones and he was playing himself.

He has dreamed this dream many times. And, though it would break his heart, he longs for it. Feels that if only he could come to the end of the dream, the end of the song, he would understand. More than this, he would be healed, though he is unsure of his wound. But, though he would play to his last breath, the end never comes. He is always interrupted.

"Veron."

Today, it is the girl. The girl from the bridge. She strides right up to him, stands full-square in the dream, and says: "Veron."

And then he's awake. Thrashing on the bed. The song in pieces. *Veron*.

This is his name. And not his name. He first saw it on the scrap of paper that did for a Chilean birth certificate. Jan Veron Veron. Written in swirling black and, next to it, a tiny thumbprint. His. They must have inked his baby hand and pressed it there. Jan Veron. He exists. He gives his permission for whatever you are about to do to him.

In Chile a child is called after both father and mother. But his father would not put a name to him, so he got double his mother's name: Jan Veron Veron. Sometimes he thinks even the "Jan" is a mistake. That they were careless at the registry (for what did it matter? What did he matter?) and so changed his forename, changed him, with a slip of a pen, from Spanish "Juan" to Dutch "Jan". But there again, maybe "Jan" was the gift of his mother, a special name that meant something to her? How can he know? All that is certain is that he has moved continents and his name has changed again. Now he is Jan Rupert Veron Spark. Is this what the argument is about? Is this what caused his mother (his English mother) to cry?

He thought he put it kindly, he thought he'd said it so she'd understand.

"I just want the Veron part of my name to be my surname."

"Instead of Spark?" The fear was white around her eyes.

"No. No." He is aware of what he owes. And besides, he loves his English mother. She must know that.

From under his pillow he takes the stump-armed Worry Doll. Violeta. She has not performed her miracle. She has not removed his worry. But that is, maybe, because she *is* the worry. Violeta Veron, his Chilean mother. He holds her in his hands. He searches for her everywhere. Not the doll of course, the mother. He looks at every Latin woman in the street, on the bus, in the cinema. He has never seen a picture of his mother, no one thought to take a photograph. But he has a picture in his head. Violeta. A violet violated. A Chilean Cinderella, dark and utterly beautiful and dressed in rags. He wants to stop searching, but he can't. She is always there, just out of reach, just around the next corner. He thought maybe if he carried part of her name, with his name, if he could become Veron-Spark, then maybe there would be some peace. It was only a hyphen he was asking for. Not a big thing, he thought.

"It would be," said his mother, "as if you were turning your back on us. Your family."

And of course they are his family. Susan Spark and her husband David. They have cared for him since he was three months old. Susan Spark has held him in her arms and poured love into him. She has sat by him nights when he woke screaming with terrors he couldn't communicate. She has never lied to him. "You are an adopted child," she told him as soon as he was old enough to hear. "Your father and I love you. We chose you. Wanted you – want you – more than life itself."

And what could his life with Violeta have been? If they had lived, that is. For nothing and no one would have guaranteed those lives. Another mother and child dead on the streets of Santiago. Who would have cared? Who would even have noticed? But perhaps they might have scraped a life, her as a maid (though his father, a white lawyer, would not have employed her in his house any more) and Jan perhaps making shoes from old tyres or, as he grew, offering his services as a male prostitute. No, he is under no illusions. But Veron is his name. That is all. Is he asking for anything that isn't his?

"Only she won't have another child," he says to his English mother (even though he knows he is not Violeta's firstborn and therefore unlikely to be her last), "and then her name, then she... she'll die."

"No," his English mother cries, "please don't ask it, Jan."

So he will not. Not again. He won't say a word. He will lock Veron inside him though it screams to be out.

He gets out of bed and picks up the panpipes. Puts his lips to the bamboo. Blows. A thin sound returns. A weak, reedy, hopeless noise. But some part of the dream is still in his head, and he is determined. It is a long while now since he bought the pipes and at least he can make a sound now. Before there was just spit and breath. He doesn't like to play in the house, which is why he goes to the bridge. Some of the sounds he is searching for are up in that loneliness. But tonight he has no choice. It is one in the morning and he cannot go to the bridge. Besides, the song is in his head. Or fragments of it. There may not come another time like this.

So he takes the pipes again, wets his lips, breathes

evenly, tries one of the longer canes, for these are more mellow, easier to play. They do not squeak and complain at being played by Jan Rupert Spark. But the music is not as it is in his head, it's just reedy noise, and he feels the anger rising. As though the pipe is resisting him, refusing him. And all the while Jan Spark's guitar looks at him from the corner of the room and laughs. No one taught him where to place his fingers on these strings, he just took the instrument and played. Simple chords, a simple strum, and the songs were right. What need you of the pipes, says the guitar, when you have me? Aren't I enough for you? I who sing so sweetly to your tune?

Jan puts down the pipes and picks up the guitar. Maybe, just maybe, if he could pick out the notes on these strings, if he could fix that haunting phrase, see where it was leading... He begins to pluck, moving his hands, finding his way. He is intent, his fingers mobile and a tune comes. It's an alluring tune, but it is not wild enough, high enough, it does not contain mountains. He tries again. And again.

"Jan."

Has he woken her?

"Jan…" His mother comes to his bedside.

Is she still angry? He looks up at her eyes. They seem hunted. Perhaps she has lain awake all this time. He is ashamed for the argument they have had. Ashamed for the hurt he has caused.

She lays a hand on his hand. "You play so beautifully."

And then he's afraid that she'll ask him once again, mention the Celeb Night, the opportunity to play in front of... No. He shakes his head. Can't she see it's not the point? Not what the music is for?

"Just come with me," she says. "Just to the restaurant on Sunday. Meet Mrs Van Day. That's all I ask. Will you, Jan?"

And it isn't much to ask. It would be simply churlish to refuse. He only has to say "yes" and she will return to bed. She will sleep. Be happy.

"Yes," he says.

"Thank you, Jan."

She leaves and then, very quietly, for he does not wish to disturb her at all, he takes up the pipes again.

He plays and plays. Plays until he is rimmed with exhaustion. Then he lays the pipes aside, gathers up stump-armed Violeta and puts her under his pillow. He is making progress. An end will come.

He sleeps.

5.

It's Sunday so I'm a bus boy. My father's brasserie has not moved into the twenty-first century, there are no bus girls here. Though, to be fair, my co-worker at the dumbwaiter is Aaron. Very much a boy. Ginger-haired and pimply, he has something wrong with his nose, so he keeps his mouth permanently open in order to breathe. Aaron and I press the dumbwaiter buttons and steaming plates of food arrive from the kitchen below. We open the lift doors, extract the plates, put them on trays and present the offerings to the rushed and impatient waitresses. In return the waitresses bring us trays of dirty dishes. We scrape the leavings into Waste Bin 1: chips, lettuce, beef fat, fish bones. We drop empty bottles into Waste Bin 2, stack the greasy crockery in the second lift. Push the buttons. Red. Green. Basement.

It's mechanical, repetitive work and it doesn't stop you thinking. Today I'm thinking about Aaron, about how, when someone finally kisses him, he'll probably die from lack of oxygen. But then I can't imagine anyone wanting to kiss Aaron so maybe he has a long life ahead after all. Plates in. Plates out. Actually, I'm not really thinking about Aaron. I'm trying not to think about Grandma, about what she said. Which is stupid, because it was days ago, the day I went to the bridge.

"Why did you do it?" she asked. "Skip school? Your father said you didn't have to go. But you wanted to. You agreed to go. So you should have gone." And then: "We can't have lying, Tilly."

Which always means, plates in, plates out, that Grandma's going to talk about my grandfather. Gerry. Wonderful, impeccable, dead Gerry. Tomatoes into Bin 1, beer bottle into Bin 2.

"Gerry never let me down. If Gerry said he'd be home at six, then he was home at six. Even if he'd had to drive six hundred miles that day. That's what integrity's all about. Honesty. Trust. Do you want me not to trust you, Tilly?"

Thai Fish out. Roast Belly of Pork out. Vegetables out.

"What have you to say for yourself, Tilly?"

More vegetables out. Poached eggs out. Surely breakfast should be off by now?

"Speak up, Tilly."

"Does being dead make people perfect, Grandma?"

"Don't be cheeky, Tilly."

"Tilly? Tilly!" It's Janey now, one of the waitresses. "Are you deaf?" Janey has a problem with the cover at Table Ten. It's a woman. She asked for soft poached eggs and the eggs are, apparently, like bullets. Janey has to go down and speak to Chef, she has to have soft eggs fast.

"Please, Tilly. Just get these drinks to Table Seven. They're screaming for them."

Buses aren't allowed to get drinks from the bar. It's against the law. But we are, when required, allowed to carry them. There are four drinks on this tray. Two tall glasses of Coca-Cola with ice and lemon, one large balloon glass of honey-coloured wine, Chardonnay probably, and one shorts glass. In this glass is a shot of vodka. Vodka on the rocks with lime and soda. And even the lime can't mask it. That thin, distilled, sweet odour that makes my heart reel.

"Tilly!"

The smell winds around my body, around and around, and up my nose.

"Tilly – for God's sake!"

Can't she see my hand is trembling? I cannot lift the tray. Cannot have that smell nearer me than it already is. No. Please no.

"Table Seven, Tilly."

"You can do it, Tilly," says Gerda. "Trust me."

I pick up the tray and I walk.

"Where on earth are the drinks?"

Jan has his eyes on Mrs Van Day so as not to have to look at Mercy. Mrs Van Day is tall and commanding. She wears a tight black bodice under an expensive suit and her nails and her lips are scarlet. She presides over the table. She directs the conversation, commandeers it, drives it like an army man might drive a Saracen tank. She is thrilled to inform Mrs Spark that not only is the sponsorship deal agreed with the local paper, but she has big news. Really Big News.

"It's confirmed. They rang me this morning. Sunday. Can you believe it? Sunday morning. The producer himself."

"Yes?" says Susan Spark.

"The producer of *Pop Idol*. He's agreed to send a scout. Yes, a scout for the programme at our little show! And of course he's not making any promises, can't say they'll choose one of our talents for the TV show but – well, you know me, Susan..."

"Marvellous," says Susan Spark. "I don't know how you do it, Gloria."

"So, Jan," says Mrs Van Day, leaning forward and giving a little laugh. "It could be you. You could be famous."

Jan manages a small smile. But he doesn't lift his head because he can feel her eyes on him. Not Mrs Van Day's, but her daughter Mercy's. She's waiting for a reaction. But what reaction can he give to "famous"? Being famous is not something to which Jan aspires. He aspires only to get through this meal, sitting beside the most beautiful girl he has ever seen, without making a fool of himself. There he's said it. Mercy Van Day – the most beautiful girl in the world. Did he say world? Yes, world probably. She's the kind of girl you see in pictures, the princess girl with the long blonde hair (Mercy's hair is short, but very blonde), the melting eyes and the perfect body. The sort of girl who always gets the prince. Only Jan is not a prince. Never has been, never will be. He doesn't say enough. Doesn't have the right words in his mouth. So the princesses walk on by. Only this one hasn't, this princess is sitting right beside him with need coming off her like sweat. He's burning up with the way she's looking at him. And she's been looking at him this way from the moment he came into the restaurant.

The Van Days were already seated when he and Susan Spark arrived. But Mrs Van Day rose, she towered.

"This is my daughter, Mercy," she said.

And he'd held out a hand, as you would to a stranger, but she wasn't a stranger, she said. They'd met before. And he'd nodded, of course, partly to validate her and partly because of the look she was giving him, a stare so intent that he was forced to drop his own gaze. And he's barely lifted his head since. But he doesn't have to. He can see her in the bright silver of the candlestick, in the shimmering curves of the glasses which wait for water. And he can smell her. That rosy white English girl skin. Bathed and soaped and perfumed but still with that musky, needy, animal tang. He swallows. His throat is parched.

"Really," says Mrs Van Day. "I've never known the service here so slow. What can they be doing? Pressing the grapes?"

"Oh look," says Jan's mother. "Here we are, I think."

A waitress comes to the table. "Vodka?" she says.

And when he hears that voice, Jan lifts his head, he looks up.

It is the girl from the bridge.

"Tilly!" Mercy exclaims.

But the girl only has eyes for Jan. Those same angry eyes she had at the bridge. As though he has no right to be in this restaurant. As though, once again, he has intruded. And he would like to say something, defend himself, or just make her relax. But what can he say? He does not know her. Yet he feels as if he knows her. Veron. She walked into his dream and knew him. When he was a tiny child and woke screaming in the night, Susan Spark said, "Hush, hush, it is only a dream." As if dreams were nothings, curls of smoke which would dissipate in the morning air. But his dreams stay with him. And the girl is in the dreams.

"Vodka," Tilly says again, as though she is biting the word.

"That's mine, dear," says Mrs Van Day.

It's then that Jan sees the doll. Or at least the doll's head. It protrudes from Tilly's apron pocket. A shining mass of black hair. And he has an urge to touch, to reach out his hand, because he has a sudden vision (perhaps a dream) of the doll as a physical pain. As if, perhaps, the girl keeps the doll as close to her as he keeps stump-armed Violeta. And, perhaps, suffers as much.

But if he moves a hand, the girl moves faster.

She bangs a glass down in front of him. Coke slops.

"Oh," exclaims Mrs Van Day.

And then, sharp as a needle, Mercy's voice says: "Do you two know each other?"

I'm back at the bus-boy station. I don't know how I unloaded those drinks from the tray. Put that glass of swirling vodka down with the boy looking, staring. The way he does. As if he knows something. Looking at me. Looking at Gerda. I saw his eyes slip right down, and I couldn't touch her, protect her, because I needed both hands for the tray, the drinks. What does he want?

Jan.

That's what she called him. Jan.

Repeating it. "Do you know Tilly, Jan?"

Her boy then. The hunted, hunting boy from the bridge is Mercy's boy. The drill-eyed hound at my back is Mercy's Inca god.

Gerda says: "Be calm."

But I am not calm. I can still feel Mrs Van Day's hand as it closed over mine.

"I'm so sorry," she said, "to hear about your mother."

Mercy's mother pitying me. Mercy's mother still alive. Sitting there at the table having lunch. With Jan and his mother. Mother and daughter. Mother and son. Two perfect families. Happy, smiling.

I'm so sorry.

So sorry.

So sorry.

"It's full," says Aaron, through his nose.

"What?"

"The rubbish bin," he says very slowly and very nasally. "You can't fit any more bottles in because it's full."

I look down. In each hand I have a beer bottle and I'm pushing, I'm forcing them down into that overflowing bin, as though I would break them, crush them, smash the glass.

"Here," says Aaron. "I'll go empty it."

"No." I heave the bin liner from the plastic container. Bottles clash and clink. "I'll do it."

"It'll be too heavy for you," says Aaron. He likes to take rubbish to the kitchen. On the way back he filches chips.

"Leave off. I'm taking it."

His need for food is strong, but not as strong as my need to be away from those happy, happy families. I lug the bin liner around the counter.

"Watch it," says Janey as I bang into her legs. But I go on, kicking the bag towards the kitchen steps. Kicking it down the steps. Clink. Clash. Clash. Clink.

The nearer I come to the bottom, the hotter it gets. Gas jets flare, ovens exhale and heat clings to the ceiling strip lights. A radio thump-thumps behind the noise of the washing-up machine.

"Kiss my arse, two roast beef," yells Chef.

Above the steel stoves extractor fans whirl uselessly. A huge vat of gravy heaves and roils.

Chef stirs a finger in a tray of Yorkshire puddings.

"These are dried sea sponges aren't they, Phil?"

I have to be careful, manoeuvre my way between the apple sauce and gravy stove and the salad preparation table. The space is narrow and the floor greasy.

"Isn't Aaron on today?" asks Phil.

I grunt.

"Does that mean you turned into Aaron?" Phil remarks.

"Can you scale your omelettes down a bit?" shouts Chef.

At the back of the kitchen, near to the entrance of the alleyway where the bottles have to go, Luca is working. Despite his Italian name, Luca is Nordic looking: big, powerful and very pale-skinned. He's flashing a knife against a steel. I hear the noise of sharpening, feel it, like the sparks were in my face. I cannot take my eyes from the flashing blade, right, left, right, left. It's a vegetable knife of course. But a restaurant one. So it's big and not unlike the long thin-bladed carving knife in my mother's house.

"Turn away," says Gerda. "Take the bottles."

Luca puts down the steel. He smiles. He's going to chop chillies. His movements are brutally swift. He cuts off the stalk end and then, holding the chilli between the finger and thumb of his left hand, slices a line from tip to gaping mouth. One perfect slit and then the seeds are scraped away, the red flesh pitilessly chopped, the knife moving with ferocious rhythm. And me not moving. Me rooted to the spot looking at the chopped red flesh, the pieces of it, falling away from his knife and thinking this, it looks like blood. Drops of blood, falling away from the knife. And I want to make it stop. I have to stop that blood, that knife.

"Pull yourself together, Tilly," says Grandmother. *"You don't know what you're talking about."*

And Gerda says: "Mama's all right. Mama loves you. She'll be better in the morning. Go now, Tilly."

But I can't go. I'm transfixed. And any minute now Luca's going to stop chopping and ask why I'm hanging around here with my mouth open.

"Aargh!" screams Luca.

He has cut himself. He has gashed the tip of his left index finger.

Bright red blood is blobbing on to the chopping board.

"It's only petals," says Gerda. "It is only petals falling. Red rose petals."

"Aah, aah, aaah," shouts Luca.

"Stupid git," says Chef.

Luca turns to the basin behind him, runs his finger under a stream of cold water.

While his back is turned, I stretch up to the chopping board. Put my finger in the blood, smear it. It smells familiar. It smells of metal. In the blood are chilli bits and chilli seeds. I scoop them up, put them in the starched white pocket of my apron. Then I take out the rubbish.

The alleyway is cool, a breeze coming down from the street above. I breathe deeply. Take a stinking lungful of rotted vegetables, stale beer, car exhaust fumes, cold stone floors.

Only petals. Just red petals. I put my hand on Gerda, around her wrist. Feel the prick of the tiny, red glass beads. The triangular point of one in my fingertip. Just red petals.

I lift the bag of bottles, push it up towards the mouth of the green wheelie bin. This wheelie bin is empty. The first of the bottles thud on to plastic, then they begin to crash and smash on top of each other. A single wine bottle jams itself into the corner of the black bag, refusing to budge. I put my hand deep inside the bag, wrest it free and fling it into the bin. It bounces, clinks, spins and settles.

I am calm now.

The bag is torn. I throw it in the ordinary rubbish and then I head back through the kitchen.

Luca's finger sports a blue plaster. He is crushing garlic, using the heel of his hand on the back of that very sharp knife. He smiles.

"Hi, Tilly," he says. "How ya doing?"

"Fine," I say.

He nods, crushes.

"Who's plating up?" yells Chef.

"Coming, Chef," says Luigi.

And I'm coming too. Up the steps and into the different hubbub of the restaurant. I will not look at Table Seven.

"Did you bring me any chips?" asks Aaron.

"No."

"I'm starving," he says plaintively. "Starving."

I busy myself stacking crockery.

"Do you know those people at Table Seven then?" Aaron asks.

"No."

"Why are they looking at you then?"

"They aren't."

"They are. At least he is. The boy. Is he your boyfriend?"

"Shut up, Aaron."

"You should have got me chips. I'd've got you chips." He scrapes lettuce into the bin. "And she's looking at you."

"Who?"

"The woman. The one with the big hair and the red nails."

Mrs Van Day looking at me and thinking what, saying what? *That poor creature, to think of that poor creature and her mother.*

"The mother who loved you," whispers Gerda.

But I hear something else, something very high and very clear, above all the noise of the restaurant. Something louder than the scrape of forks and knives, and the conversational din, something that cuts right through low music and the whisper of my beloved and it is one word.

"Darling."

And I can't really have heard her say it, because she is so far away. But I'm looking now and there she is, Mrs Van Day leaning across to her daughter, and her body language says it too. "Darling. My darling." And Mercy smiles, she opens, blossoms there in the gaze of her mother. Her mother who loves her right now. Her mother who is alive.

Ping! The dumbwaiter speaks. Food for Table Seven, it says. And I know what I will do.

"No," says Gerda.

But I have my hand in my pocket and I'm scraping out those chilli bits and those hot, hot chilli seeds and that smear of Luca's blood. Why else would I have brought them? And I'm lifting the white flesh of the fish.

"No," says Gerda.

I know they are having fish, mother and daughter, because I saw the fish knives and forks when I went to the table. The beef must be for Jan and his mother. But the fish... Beneath the fillet is a soft run of juices and it's there that I tuck the red choppings and the yellow seeds and those petals of Luca's blood.

"What are you doing?" asks Aaron.

"Janey asked me to take this," I say. And I push Gerda down, because she's moving in my apron pocket.

I load the plates on to a tray and then I'm off, gliding, very calmly, across the chequered floor to Table Seven.

Jan is at home, upstairs in his room. It is cool here and quiet. He can breathe. Though he will not, he thinks, be alone long. The women are downstairs. His mother and Mrs Van Day, sitting in the drawing room, retelling the story of the restaurant. Getting the details right: the look on Tilly's face, the choking, the fracas, the arrival of Tilly's father (summoned from his office by the restaurant manager). The generous, extenuating pity.

"Of course it's to do with the poor girl's mother."

Mercy is sitting downstairs too. Talking, joining in as required. But also waiting. She has, he thinks, something to say, something private. So she will follow him. Yes. He is expecting her. Her smell still in his nostrils. Sweet and bitter and sexy.

Meanwhile, there is a little time and he needs that time. The doll will rest no longer. Tilly's doll. He has it in his pocket. While she was poised with the tray, he put his hand around that mass of black doll hair and pulled. There was no resistance at all. The doll just slid out of Tilly's apron and into his trouser pocket. It was a silent thing, though his heart pounded.

He takes the doll out now and puts it in the palm of his hand. It lies there like a stiff star, its arms and legs pulled away from its trunk. Its blue sequin eyes staring unseeing at the ceiling. It is bland, inert. He fingers it gently, its various skins, the black leather and the white, the coloured velvets. Nothing.

What did he expect? That the doll would move, rear up? Speak to him? Yield its secrets just because he was looking?

He touches again. This time stroking the stitches, the ugly black slashes about the doll's white throat. Stitches that, at a distance, made him feel that this doll was a wound. More than this, that the doll was evil. The incubus that drove the girl to take her life in her hands at the bridge, who willed her to push burning seeds into the mouths of the Van Days. At the doll's ankles are similar stitches, large, misshapen, but not hideous. No. Close to, the stitching seems merely desperate. Sad even. As though a child had made this doll, under duress, punching the needle in and out, not caring about the colour of the cotton or the size of the stitches, just wanting the job done, finished. But that's not right either, because there is love in this doll too. The big, smiling (if lopsided) mouth, the soft and many coloured velvets, the red bracelet. The tiny glass beads painstakingly assembled, although the elastic is too tight. It bites into the white flesh of the doll's wrist.

Jan does not understand. He concentrates, conjures again the girl's face, reconstructs her fury. The way she looked at him up at the bridge, as though he was an intruder. And then again, at the restaurant table, the same look, an anger which made him feel... what? At fault. As though she both hated and required something of him. And so he'd acted. Pulled the doll from her pocket as he might have pulled the key from a maddened piece of clockwork. Thinking that he could make it stop. Make her stop. Unwind.

"What's it to do with you!" she might have shouted again. But she didn't. Just spun silently on her heels, untied her apron (so maddened she didn't even notice the absence of the doll?), and walked out the door of the restaurant and away down the street. He'd watched her go. She's fleeing, he thought (though she wasn't running), fleeing, just like she did at the bridge.

"*You live too much in your imagination,*" his English mother says, though he is alone in the room. "*There are things which are true — and then there are stories.*"

Jan looks out of his bedroom window. In a few hours it will be dark. Stars will shine. And it will be impossible to know whether those stars are living or dead. Because dead stars still shine, the light they give out before they expire taking maybe a thousand years to reach the earth. Is that just a story? No. It is a truth. You have to understand with your heart as well as look with your eyes.

But he still should not have taken the doll. How would it be if she had leaned over and stolen Violeta? The idea alone quickens his breath, makes him reach out to the drawer and the tiny box, just to check that his stump-armed Violeta is safe. She is safe. He closes the box, slides the drawer shut.

There is a knock at the door.

He closes his hand over Tilly's doll.

Mercy's face appears. "Did I make you jump?"

He shakes his head.

"Do you mind me coming in?"

She comes in.

She is composed now. Her face, once more, flawless skin. In the restaurant he saw sinew, bone. As she bit into the chilli seeds her face contorted, her neck twisting with the effort of swallowing. Then her head began to shake. Her hair swinging in a frenzied staccato, cracking the tang of her about him like a whip. Then the spitting started. She grabbed for water, took huge gulps, crying out the while so that the water spilled from her mouth. His mother thrust her a napkin and she fought to clean herself, to wipe away the shame. But the fire in her mouth was too violent, so she had to take more water, more and more until she vomited it on to her plate, her fish a lake of spat fluid. The mothers were shocked. His own mother offered napkins and consolation, but Mrs Van Day roared, all indignation until her own teeth closed on a seed and the burn began to burst on her lips too. She moaned, she cried, then she grabbed for her daughter and hurtled them both towards the ladies' loo.

The commotion excited the other diners. All eyes

swivelled to the table where he and his mother sat, now silent and exposed. The mood was expectant, as though someone (himself, his mother?) was about to make an announcement, offer an explanation. But what explanation could there be? For an unbearable minute, they sat and sat and then the restaurant manager arrived, swiftly followed by Richard Weaver, the restaurant owner. A small sandy man with a soothing voice, Tilly's father offered apologies and astonishment. He couldn't imagine how it had happened, he was taken aback and sincere.

It took Mrs Van Day to mention Tilly. Mrs Van Day who returned at length from the ladies, all make-up wiped from her lips. "But think nothing of it," she said to Mr Weaver's further apologies (he had checked the facts with a bus boy). In the light of the tragic circumstances, Mrs Van Day said, she understood. She understood perfectly.

Mr Weaver ordered fresh linen and new main courses. But the Van Days and the Sparks could not be persuaded to stay for dessert, for coffee, for liqueurs (even though it was on the house). The Van Days and the Sparks were busy people. They needed to get away. They had things to do. Things to discuss. Like Tilly's mother.

An hour or so later they were ensconced in his mother's very English drawing room, the coffee freshly brewed.

"How many times is it now, Mercy?" asked Mrs Van Day.

"Three," said Mercy.

"I thought twice?"

"Three times."

"How can you be so sure?"

"Because every time her mother goes in the sin-bin—"

"Detox clinic, darling."

"Tilly's gran brings her to school. But her gran doesn't drive her to the gate. Too embarrassed apparently. Drops her about three roads away. Makes her walk."

"The poor girl," said Susan Spark. "The poor, poor girl."

"Still," said Mrs Van Day. "No need to take it out on Mercy. What would be the justification for that?"

Was it then that Jan left the room, mumbling something that might have meant he needed to relieve some bodily function? But he came to his room, and now Mercy has come. As he knew she would. He looks at her beautiful mouth. The chilli seeds were like nettle stings on her lips, she said.

"What is it with these seeds?" Mercy says. "What part of them stays on your hands? I just rubbed my eye and hey presto – sting sting sting. So I've just had to wash again," she adds, as if it's an explanation for her being upstairs.

The skin of her eyelids is pale and transparent. He can see thin blue veins. How delicate she is, he thinks.

"I'm sorry," she says then, "about – well, the restaurant."

"Sorry?"

"You must have thought..."

He thought nothing, just watched the way her face dissolved to bone.

"You know, it can't have been pleasant to watch."

And this is it, of course, her fear, the thing she wants to say. She is afraid that she lost control. That she looked ugly. But, even contorted, Mercy's face could not be ugly.

He shrugs. "Not your fault," he says inadequately. But how can he talk about beauty and bone?

There's a pause and then Mercy asks: "Do you know her, then? Tilly?"

What is he to say? He has seen the girl but not met her. Been addressed by her but made no reply. She walks in his dreams.

"Only the way she looked at you..."

"No," he says, "I do not know her." The words are true, but not true. They sound like a betrayal.

Something in Mercy's body seems to relax. She smiles. "I've known her for ever. We used to be friends. Good friends, in fact. In the days when she was charmingly eccentric as opposed to seriously weird."

He waits. Perhaps he was wrong. Perhaps this is what Mercedes Van Day has come to say.

"Not that it was ever an 'equal' friendship, even at the beginning," Mercy continues. "She was always a little, well, secretive. Kept something back. And, of course, she never invited me to her place. Even though she came to my house quite often. I never knew why. Until I called on her unexpectedly one day."

He says nothing, but his head is lifted.

"She tried to stop me coming in. Said her mum was asleep. 'Don't worry,' I said, 'we can tiptoe.' Well, we did tiptoe, right past her mum who was lying on the sofa in the drawing room. Then there was a moan, and a sort of choking noise and then her mother rolled off the sofa and landed on the floor. In a puddle of her own vomit." Mercy pauses. "It was disgusting. And do you know the worst thing? Her mother never even moved. Just lay there. Where she'd landed. Anyway, afterwards Tilly denied it happened. Said I'd made it up. Called me 'a filthy liar'. Said that at school, in front of everyone." She smiles again. "I'm afraid our friendship took a bit of a downhill turn after that."

Mercy crosses the room to where Jan's guitar is standing against the wall. She strums a finger across the strings.

"Are you going to play at the Celeb Night?" she asks.

Jan shrugs.

"You should. Your mum says you're amazing."

He winces.

Mercy laughs. "Go on. I'll put money on you."

"Mercy!" It's Mrs Van Day calling. "We need to go. Cindy's coming!"

Mercy looks at her watch. "Oh – the dressmaker."

Jan gets up and as he does so, Mercy catches sight of something in his hand.

"What's that?" she asks. "Oh God, it's not the doll is it? Oh, it is, let's see then."

And she's right beside him now, and when he doesn't open his hand, she touches him. Or maybe she touches the doll's hair, and just glances her fingertip against his. He feels it in his spine, like electricity.

His hand opens.

"Oh," she breathes. "Is that gross or what!" She pokes at the doll with fascinated disgust. "I'm beginning to think our friend might need some professional help. I mean that is revolting. I can't believe her mother made it."

"Her mother?" queries Jan.

"Yes, that's what Tilly's mother does, when she's not drunk. Makes dolls and sells them at markets. But they're normally big dolls, you know, rag ones. For kids. But this one – she must have been in the middle of some seriously random nightmare to have made this." Her cat eyes shine. "How did you get it?"

"When she came to the table," Jan falters. "She had it in her apron pocket. It... fell. I picked it up."

"Tilly'll be mad without it," Mercy says. "She's obsessional like that. Do you want me to take it? Give it back to her at school tomorrow?"

And he doesn't. All of a sudden he doesn't even want Mercy to touch the doll. The doll is something between him and the girl at the bridge. But Mercy is right. He shouldn't have taken it. Tilly, mad with the doll, will be madder without it.

"Mercy!" shouts Mrs Van Day.

"Jan!" shouts Mrs Spark.

"OK," Jan says. "OK." And he gives Mercy the doll.

She pushes the doll so deep inside her skirt pocket it disappears. He cannot see the bulge of it against her svelte body.

She turns to leave.

I have done wrong, he thinks.

7

I'm sitting at my mother's sewing machine, my feet on the treadle. I've lit some incense, nag champa from Bangalore. It took me a while to find the incense holder, the simple wooden stand Inti gave her. I discovered it eventually, clean and in a drawer. Grandma's work. My mother always lit incense when she worked. And sang. "*Pluie d'amour*, my soul dances in your eyes. *Pluie d'amour*." I turn the hand wheel of the machine and begin paddling with my feet. It's as I remember it, that rhythmic, comforting clunk, the background noise of my childhood. *Pluie d'amour*, my soul dances in your eyes.

"What is it?" my father asked once. "That tune?"

"Big's theme," my mother replied and laughed.

Big.

That was my mother's market name. All the traders had nicknames, not that I understood that at first. For years I thought the dun, wiry man who sold honey and mead and beeswax candles really was called Wasp. Just as I believed that Sir Henry, the second-hand clothes man (a public-school boy who bought his wares by the hundredweight, threw most of them away and still made the best profit – so he said – in the market) was a genuine member of the nobility.

Clunk, clunk-de-clunk. This machine is spooling memories as it once spooled thread. Inti. Was that a nickname? I don't think so. It was probably just strange enough for the other traders not to have to invent something new for him. Inti with his gappy teeth and Latin grin. Inti who looked out for me when my mother was busy with a customer, when she was loading or unloading. Inti who made the time pass by telling me stories about the fire inside a Mexican opal, or showing me how to blow a run of notes on the panpipes, or pointing out the flies in his new delivery of amber.

"This one," he'd say, cradling a large honey-coloured drop with an eternally dancing fly inside, "this I give to your mother." He charged her half what he wrote on the tickets for his stall. "But hey," he would shrug, "not everyone wears amber the way Big does."

Big.

Does it all come down to this? Big. Was Big a nickname or just a description? I don't know. Maybe it was simply a truth. For Big was Big in the same way that earth is earth or sky is sky. A big woman with a big laugh. Someone you remembered. Someone to be reckoned with. As much part of the market as the steel stalls, Big was essential, Big belonged. Big was big, her status clear. The only woman the male traders allowed to play the Football Game. And probably the only one who would have wanted to.

It was Sir Henry who started it.

I treadle faster.

"Reckon we've got a centre forward," Sir Henry'd shout, if he spotted an attractive woman near his stall. Centre forwards were always dark. If it was a blonde (I was eight before I realised this) he'd yell, "Striker."

Then all the other men – and Big – would pause, look up and admire the passing goods.

A bit later he might shout, "Midfielder, what do you think?" The aim of the game was to assemble a full team by the end of the day.

"Goalkeeper, more like," Wasp would remark.

"Nah," said Inti. "On the bench."

"On the transfer list, I'd say," said Big.

And they'd all laugh and Sir Henry would go to the off-licence and bring back a bottle of plonk. It would be eleven in the morning and they'd need it by then. That was Sir Henry's view. It could be cold at the market and, if it rained and the tarpaulins weren't tight, a gust of wind might gush a freezing roof-pool of water down your neck. Didn't a person standing alone against the elements deserve some comfort? It was always too rainy, or too cold, or too hot. "So hot, you could die of thirst," said Sir Henry, bringing the bottle back concealed in a plastic bag. The game with the plonk (for everything was a game at the market) was to guess the country of origin. If you guessed right, you didn't have to pay your share. If you guessed wrong, you paid for Sir Henry's.

Sometimes there were arguments about accuracy. You couldn't just say "France" – you'd have to name a region: Bordeaux, Rhône. I learnt more about regions in Europe from Sir Henry than I did from school. But Big wasn't always so patient.

"Quit haggling," she'd say. "Just get the cork out."

"You've got your own nip, haven't you?" Wasp, who enjoyed the haggling more than the wine, would retort.

And she had. A little silver flask she kept in her hip pocket. But then so did Sir Henry. And Inti. You couldn't always leave the stall. They took food and drink, all of them. Even I had a sandwich box and a Dalmatian flask of Ribena. I went so often with her, I was the market kid. They all knew me, looked out for me. Though it was Inti I loved.

Inti admired my mother's craftsmanship. He'd examine a new doll (there were always new lines), hold it, run his hands over it, comment on the stitching.

"Big," he'd murmur. "But what hands! What skill!"

Was he in love with her? I don't know. I stop treadling. I think maybe I was just in love with her, and alert to any mirror that seemed to reflect that love.

I'm aware of eyes. In the boxes lined up against the wall, the market dolls stare. Two Hallowe'en witches, with black hair and black eyes. Six of Big's top-selling "My Baby" dolls, with the Velcro strip across their pink breasts, so the customer could attach the name of their choice. If she took a liking to a customer, Big would embroider a name to order, otherwise she'd just say,

"No Tiffany? Now there's a shame." In a box labelled "Christmas" are some chubby-faced babies in red and white fur hoods. Next to this is the Nursery Rhyme box, with a half-finished Bo Peep and two pairs of Jack and Jill dolls. But it's into the plastic container marked "Fairy Tales" that I push a tentative hand. In here is a Cinderella, a Tinkerbell and two Prince Charmings. The Prince Charmings never sold very well. But she kept making them. "The triumph of hope over expectation," she said. I turn over a Rapunzel, and then I feel the velvet skirt of a Red Riding Hood.

"Get your grubby fingers off," my mother says. *"They're to sell."*

But today, I don't get my fingers off, I slide my hands deeper, lift Red Riding Hood's skirt. And there it is, the cold, glassy shape my furtive fingers expect. I pull my hand out immediately, as though I'm in the wrong, as though I've unscrewed the lid from the bottle and let that twisting, reeling smell escape. My cheek are flushed, I know they are. I'm hot, guilty. I wait for someone to come in and catch me. But no one comes. Not even Grandma. Don't you know about the Red Riding Hood skirts, Grandma? Don't you?

"Mama's sick. Mama's not well. She'll be better in the morning."

Then I want to be away from this room. I push my way out and along the landing, past my mother's bedroom. The door is shut. But it shouldn't be shut, not against me. I turn the handle, let myself in and make straight for her clothes cupboard. I need to smell my mother, bury my face in her. I open the wardrobe door. It's empty. A rail with a few wire hangers and a huge space. No clothes. Not one dress, not a skirt, not a blouse, not a pair of trousers. Nothing. Nothing at all. Except the smell of wood polish.

Grandma.

Grandma!

And now she's here, standing behind me in the doorway, watching.

"You've thrown them away," I shout. "You've thrown all the clothes away. How could you do that?"

"They were cut," says Grandma. "You know that."

And of course she's right. "You still shouldn't have done it," I say. "You should have left things."

"Maybe I've left too many things," she says. "Over the years."

I turn my back on her, yank open my mother's underwear drawer. This drawer has been spared. It springs with socks and knickers and stockings my mother never wore. I select a thick pair of black towelling socks. Though my mother was big she had tiny feet and poor circulation. Her feet were always cold. When it was really icy outside she'd come home and ask me to bring her a bowl of tepid water. She'd take off her socks, sometimes three pairs, and plunge her feet into the warmth. As her feet thawed, tears would run down her cheeks. I didn't understand it was pain, I thought it was her heart melting.

I also extract a pair of knickers, plain cotton, white once but now grey, the elastic stretched and giving. I clutch my trophies to my face, inhale. And there she is again, the perfume of her, powdered flesh, jasmine, conkers...

"Tilly," Grandma begins but is, in turn, interrupted by the doorbell.

Neither of us move. The doorbell rings again. And I know who it is. The ring is angry. It's furious. And the next thing we hear is a key in the lock. Because of course he still has a key, even after all these years. Though, out of courtesy, he normally waits for the door to be opened to him.

My grandmother goes out on to the landing.

"Richard," she says.

"Tilly," he yells and he bounds up the stairs. "Tilly, Tilly!" He barges past Grandma. "What the hell do you think you were playing at?"

"What the hell do *you* think you're playing at?" says Grandma, swift to defend me. I wish I loved her more.

My father pauses, he comes to a stop. Not because of what Grandma has said, but because he finally sees me, standing in my mother's room with some socks and a pair of knickers clutched to my face.

"Have you gone mad?" he says.

"Well, she'd have every right," says Grandma.

"You keep out of this," says my father.

"Oh," says Grandma as if he's punched her. "Oh." She sits down on the bed. "You wouldn't speak to me like that if Gerry were alive. You wouldn't dare. He wouldn't let you."

"Well?" says my father, looking at me.

I say nothing. I don't move the socks and I don't move the knickers.

"Well what?" says Grandma, recovering a little. "What are you talking about? Will somebody please let me know what's going on."

"Yes," says my father. "Why don't you, Tilly? Tell

your grandma what you consider acceptable behaviour in my restaurant."

Grandma waits.

I say nothing.

The nothing infuriates my father. His breathing is noisy.

"*The trouble with you, Richard, is you always go off at the deep end.*" That's my mother speaking – her calm voice. The one that made him even madder.

"Right," says my father. "Looks like I'm going to have to tell you, Margaret. My daughter, your granddaughter, thinks it's appropriate to put blood and glass and chilli seeds—"

"Not glass," I say from behind the knickers.

"Oh – so you admit the other two—"

"What," interrupts Grandma, "are you talking about? Blood and chilli seeds and glass what? In what?"

"In the food of my guests, my patrons. So that they choke. So that they vomit. So that I have to apologise. Explain. Although there is no explanation. Unless," he continues, "you count like mother like daughter." He comes over to me, shakes me by the shoulder. "Well," he says, "well?" He drags my hand from my face. The knickers fall to the floor.

"Leave my mother out of this," I say.

"I'd like to. I'd really like to leave Judith out of this. But there's a genetic connection, you see. A particular brand of impetuosity, of self-indulgence. Like you think you can do whatever you want whenever you want to and hang the consequences. As if only little people have to bother about consequences."

He does look little. Standing there, red and angry.

"*Small body — small mind,*" says my mother.

"I think that's enough, Richard," says Grandma.

"No it's not enough. Not nearly enough. Because do you know what the consequence of this particular lunacy is — apart from the free meals and the free drinks, that is? It's that I had to buy two tickets for that stupifyingly stupid Celeb Night event. And have you any idea what those tickets cost?"

"They're in a good cause, Richard."

"Right..." He pulls two large floppy tickets from his trouser pocket. "National Society for the Prevention of Cruelty to Children," he reads. "Yes, I see your point. Because they're going to have a big job to do in this house if you don't adjust your behaviour, Tilly M. Weaver."

When I was small enough to climb on his lap and he was shouting, I could sometimes defuse things with a smile. Not a defiant smile; an enquiring, hopeful, complicitous one. He'd sometimes catch that smile and something would change, break. He'd laugh.

I try a smile.

"And wipe that smirk off your face. You're just like her. Think everything can be laughed off. Who cares? Well, I care Tilly. I've got a business to run. A business that pays for everything you eat and everything you have."

He says it like he means "and everything you are too". Like he owns me. I stop smiling.

"I hate you," I say, very quietly, like she might have done.

"Fine," he says. "Dandy. I'm not particularly enamoured of you right now either. But I'm going to get more impressed soon because you're just about to do something responsible, something decent for a change. You're going round to Mrs Van Day's house to apologise."

"Mrs Van Day!" exclaims Grandma. "It was Mrs Van Day?"

"And Mercy," says my father. "Which is why Tilly's on her way round to their house. Right now."

"No," I say.

"Yes," he says. "Oh yes." His hands are on my shoulders. "Come on." He frogmarches me down the stairs and along the hall, pausing at the door only long enough to haul it open, shove me out and slam it behind me.

As I stand on the doorstep (it's cold, getting dark and I have no coat) I hear raised voices behind me.

"You're taking things too far," says Grandma.

"I'm sorry Margaret, but I have responsibilities. Unless someone starts drawing some boundaries Tilly's going to wind up in exactly the same place as Judith. If she can't exercise some self-control, then someone has to exercise some on her behalf. She has to learn there are lines you can cross and lines you can't. Something Judith never quite..."

I step away from the house then, because I do not want to hear it any more. My mother fouled in my father's mouth. As I begin to walk I find my right hand in my right pocket. I'm reaching for Gerda.

But, of course, Gerda isn't there.

8

Gerda's in my apron pocket. I left her there. Folded inside a neat square of cloth at the restaurant. Grandma's right. I do have a temper. A boiling rage that erupts, just like my father's. But also a cold anger that makes me go very still inside. It frightens me, how detached I can feel, how I felt when Gerda (my joy, my beloved) whispered that one word to me:

"No."

So I forgot her. I just walked away. I've practised this over the years. I can refuse things, lock them in boxes, make them safe. Sometimes I think my brain is full of locked boxes. And that one day there will be too many boxes and my brain will explode. Then fourteen years of scary things will cascade to the floor and finally I'll have to look. But not now. Not yet. That's how I've survived. Until now. Until my father came and said what he said and I dipped my hand in my pocket and Gerda wasn't there.

And I felt a hole open up in me bigger than my heart. Like I was empty and could never be full again.

Which is why I turn left (towards the restaurant) and not right (towards Mercy's) at the bottom of the drive.

"Where are you going, Madam?"

Somehow my father has emerged from the house. He has caught up with me. More than this, he's standing in front of me, blocking my way.

"I'm going back to work," I say. "I'm sorry I clocked off early."

"Did you hear anything in there?" he asks. "Anything at all?"

I wait.

"Get in the car," he says. He points at the machine as if I don't understand English.

I don't move.

"Get in the car."

I go back up the drive and get in the car. He follows me, climbs in, slams his hand on the door lock and roars out of the drive. Exactly seven minutes later (I'm watching the clock so as not to have to look at him) he jerks up in front of Mercy's house.

"Out," he says.

I get out. Stand on the pavement.

"Doorbell," he says.

I go up to the door. It's almost a year since I stood here last. They have a new knocker. A brass fish.

"Knock," says my father.

I put my hand in my pocket. Gerda isn't there.

"Knock!" he says. "Damn you."

I knock.

Mrs Van Day opens the door.

"Oh," she says, "Tilly..."

My father leans out of the car. "Tilly has something to say to you," he shouts. Then he shuts his door and drives away.

"Oh," repeats Mrs Van Day. And then, into my silence: "Do you want to come in, Tilly?"

"I'm sorry," I say then. And I am. How is Mrs Van Day to blame? "Very sorry." The words feel physical, like scented oil on skin. It'll be like this when I apologise to Gerda. She will look at me out of those blue eyes, I'll say sorry and she'll forgive me. It'll be all right. "About the restaurant." I add. "I don't know what came over me."

Mrs Van Day draws me over the threshold. "Tilly,"

she says, "Tilly," she sighs and puts her hand on mine. "It's not important. Doesn't matter at all. What's important is... is there anything we can do?"

"I need to see Mercy."

"Of course. Cindy's here, though. Dress-fitting. Well, trouser-fitting actually. But..." She looks at my face. "She's in the drawing room. Just go in, you know your way. I'm making tea. Do you want one?"

I never drink tea. But as this is the first time today anyone has offered me anything, I say, "Thank you. Thank you very much."

She turns towards the kitchen and I cross the hall to the drawing room. I can hear voices. I push the door very gently because I need the room to be just as I remember it. A serene room with white sofas and a white carpet. And yes, here it is. Above the white marble fireplace, the bevelled glass mirror in the plain gold frame. At the windows, the watered cream silk curtains with the pale gold tiebacks. And yes, yes – to my right – the enfolding white sofa in which I lay that Saturday when Mercy, who'd arranged to meet me at two o'clock, didn't turn up till five.

"I'd just go home if I were you," said Mrs Van Day. "Teach the wretch a lesson."

But I loved lying there, could have lain there all day and all night. It seemed such a clean, calm room. Compared, at least, with my house where even the colours and patterns clash and shout. I remember thinking, as I lay there dozing, nothing bad could ever happen in this room.

"Tilly!"

Mercy is standing in the centre of the room. She's wearing a breast-hugging bodice of slashed white and pale blue which covers her back but exposes her taut stomach and the beautiful hollow of her tummy button. At her hips is a wide white belt from which blue gauze trousers flow. The trousers are quite transparent and beneath them she wears a pair of blue satin shorts cut high on her thighs like a bikini bottom. At the hem of her left leg, Cindy kneels. She has a mouth full of pins which she's extracting from a small doll-shaped pincushion on the floor.

Only it's not a pincushion. It's Gerda.

"Let me guess," says Mercy. "You've come to apologise. It was all a big mistake. You don't know what came over you – again. You're really sorry."

Cindy looks up. "Hi," she says through the pins.

Gerda says nothing. Her blue eyes stare at the

ceiling. There are pins in her right arm, her left arm, her legs, at her throat, at her breast, through her heart. And I want it not to be true. I want my eyes to be lying to me, so I just stand there, immobile, waiting for the picture to change. Because there is no way Gerda can be here. No way that she can be lying on this floor, stabbed through. No way at all.

"Well?" says Mercy, shifting her weight.

"Keep still," mouths Cindy.

Mercy moves but I keep still, I don't move a muscle. Just watch as Cindy, using the last of pins in her mouth, stretches a hand towards Gerda and pulls a thin steel blade from Gerda's hip. The force of the extraction is enough to spin Gerda, twist her. So now she's facing me, looking up at me. Her eyes are blank.

That unlocks me. "Gerda!" I scream.

"Gerda," Mercy says. "Gerda, eh?" And I know she's smiling. I can feel it on my back. I'm on the floor, crawling, grabbing at Gerda, lifting her, pulling those pins out of her body. But I'm too angry and my fingers are all fumble. I start at her heart, trying to get five or six pins out at a time, but I'm jerking, shaking, and there's still one there, and two at her throat. And I want to pull with both hands, but I also want to hold her, press her against my heart, because only then will I know. But it's all taking so very long. "How could you!" I cry.

"Gosh," says Cindy, taken aback. "I mean, I didn't..." She looks helplessly up at Mercy.

"It's only a doll," says Mercy.

All the pins are out. But Gerda is still limp, lifeless. I clutch her at last to my breast. Nothing. Nothing at all. "Speak to me!" I yell.

"Dolls don't speak," says Mercy. "They're inanimate objects. They have stuffing where you and I have brains. Well, where I have a brain, anyway."

"I don't understand," says Cindy.

"No, you wouldn't," says Mercy. "You see it really doesn't make much sense. But it's probably to do with genes and madness."

"You took her. You stole her!"

"Not exactly," Mercy says. "You dropped her. Jan picked her up. Her! What's with this 'her' stuff? You dropped IT. It! That thing. That creepy thing. Jan picked it up. I said I'd return it." She pauses. "And now I have."

"You stuck pins in her."

"We needed a pincushion."

"Pins in her stomach, pins in her throat!"

"Yes?"

"And in her heart!"

"OK."

"You've killed her!"

"Ah right. Emergency. Call the Doll Police."

Mrs Van Day comes in with a tea tray set with a silver teapot and four china cups. "Everything all right?" she says.

"It will be," Mercy says, "if you've got the number of the funny farm."

"I'm sorry?" says Mrs Van Day.

"Tilly's of the opinion that I've murdered her doll. But I'm not sure it will stand up in court."

Mrs Van Day looks at me. "Tilly," she says, "Tilly, do you want me to phone your grandma?"

"No," I cry. "No, no, no."

And then I run, out of that room and out of that house and out along the street.

"Tilly..." Mrs Van Day calls after me.

But I don't look back. Just run north, north towards the railway line, towards the place that Gerda first took me, our place. The place she wanted me to be when she whispered that first word, "Come." If anywhere on earth can restore her it will be here, this wasteland, this bridge. There is something in the air there. You can breathe. Gerda will breathe again. So I run and I hold her close, as if my heart could start hers.

It's getting dark. When I arrive at the bridge, I fling myself down by an elderflower bush. The ground is damp. From behind me I hear the noise of a train.

"Trust me, trust me, trust me."

"Gerda."

Nothing.

"Gerda!"

Still nothing.

"I'm sorry. I'm so sorry."

Nothing.

So I inhale, I take a huge lungful of that high, wasteland air. Then I close my mouth over Gerda's and breathe out, as if I could force breath into her, kiss her back to life.

Nothing.

Then I see it. In the side of her neck, a last pin. It's buried deep, right up to the head, which is why I have missed it. And I get my nail under this one last cruelty and I pull. Pull. Pull. And it's out.

Then I hold my own breath as I wait and wait (as I waited for my mother) for Gerda to breathe again.

But she does not.

9

Jan is up at the bridge. He's come to fill his lungs with air and blow into the pipes. It's dusk, and as he listens to the tune of the Antara and the sound of his own breath, a thought fidgets his mind: there is no new air on the planet, no virgin breath, only what's been recycled, shared. As he inhales, he imagines atoms of oxygen flowing through his body, atoms which he blows out (through the pipes) as carbon dioxide and which the plants around him (the elderflower, the cow parsley, the dock leaves) accept in their turn, breathing in his carbon dioxide only to exhale it back into the world as oxygen. This means, he thinks, that the air he is breathing now will have passed through the lungs of the long-dead, and who knows whose lungs those might have been? Confucius's, Mozart's, Hitler's? Or perhaps this breath once belonged to a lion, or a mouse or a wombat, and returned to him via a nettle or a giant redwood tree. He must be careful of this breath, he realises, for he also breathes it for the yet unborn.

And for his mother.

For this is where the thought is leading. To Violeta Veron. She lives close to the rainforests which breathe for the world, whose air the wind lifts across seas and continents. So perhaps this very inhalation has come round the world from her, and, even now, it is beginning its long return journey. And thus they are still bound to each other, just as they were when she held him in her arms at the moment of his birth.

He is so involved in this thought, and the tune which is coming from the pipe (which has a tenderness he has not previously achieved), that it is some while before he looks as well as listens. And when he looks this is what he sees: a girl kneeling on the wet ground, head bowed over a task. The task is drawing a thin, shiny object (a pin? A needle?) across the inside of her left wrist. The track of the pin is marked by a line of small, bright blobs of blood, strung together like a bead bracelet. There are two or three of these bracelets running parallel across her wrist. The girl is Tilly. She observes the red bracelets without emotion, and then she moves the pin, pushing it harder, jabbing it into a blood spot, pulling at the flesh, lifting it, making this one wound wider and deeper. The jabs are fierce, but she appears quite calm, maybe she even smiles, as though there is relief in this blood-letting.

Jan's pipes hang about his neck. He has stopped playing, he has almost stopped breathing. Is he to stand by and watch Tilly injure herself? But she is not suffering, at least not suffering from the blood. So he does just stand there. After all, he's interfered before and she has run away. And he does not want her to run again. He wants to talk with her. No, he wants to hold her. This is the feeling surging through him, he wants to take her in his arms, press her close and feel the bloodied beat of her heart against his own. But he makes no move at all.

Where the deeper cut is, the blood is forming into a fat drop, heavy enough to fall under its own weight. The slightest turn of her wrist, or dip of her arm, and gravity would have that drop, bring it to earth. But Tilly keeps her hand flat, poised, making the blood work at falling, watching its slow but inexorable gathering and pooling. And it's while she waits that she must, at last, feel his eyes on her. Because she looks up suddenly, sees him and screams.

It is not a scream of surprise or shock, a small thing quickly over. It's a long, open-throated yell. The noise is huge. It fills the wasteland. A noise to tremble plants and deafen trains. Her mouth a giant screaming O. And he wants it, needs it, to stop. So he throws himself to the ground and grabs her by the wrists (does he also want to put his finger across that blood, stop that too?). She struggles, pulls against him, but he is strong, he can hold her, but he cannot hold the noise. It spirals, it goes up a pitch, two pitches, which makes him feel afraid. Her face is very close to his, her eyes dark and staring, her mouth howling wide. His heart crashes in his chest. And still the noise comes out of her, as though she doesn't have to breathe, as though she can scream for ever. And he has to put an end to it.

If he had another hand, he would put it across her mouth. But he only has two hands and they are around her wrists. So he leans forward and clamps his mouth over hers. Takes that scream in his own throat and swallows it.

The noise stops. Her lips are wet, sweet, strange. The two of them hang together a moment there, and then she pulls away, panting. Immediately he releases her wrists.

He thinks she might hit him, raise her fists and batter his head. That would be all right. What would it matter if she hurt him? He wouldn't move. He would just kneel there and let her do it. But she sits back down on her heels, draws away from him, pulls down her shirt sleeve and buttons it at the cuff. So the wounds are gone, disappeared.

Then she looks at him and says, as though nothing at all has happened: "You should tune those pipes." If she sees his astonishment she does not pause. "In the winter, when they're cold, they play too low. You have to put seeds in them. Pulses. Just a few, six maybe. Ten. That's what Inti did. Makes the pipes play better."

This is not the conversation he expected, and certainly not the one he wants to have. Which is about the girl, her mother, the doll, the wounds buttoned up under the cuff. And also about the kiss. For he has kissed her, hasn't he?

"Why do you always come?" she asks then. "Wherever I am, you come."

But this is his place. He owes her no explanation for being up at his bridge.

"Who are you?"

Oh – to answer that. He is an English boy born in Chile. A boy with Chilean blood raised in cold rain. An orphan who yet has a mother, two mothers. A boy who lives too much in his heart, in his imagination, and whose words – like now – stick in his throat. A dreamer on the edge of love, for it is love (isn't it?) that he feels for this girl?

"And why did you take Gerda?" This is sudden and more aggressive. "Give her to Mercy? Why did you do that? Mercy stuck pins in her. Pins in her stomach, her head, her heart. So she can't talk any more. Doesn't talk to me." She pulls the doll out of her pocket, thrusts it towards him. "See?"

The doll lies limply on the palm of her hand. Tilly withdraws her then, strokes the side of the doll's face. "She had my mother's voice."

He leans a little towards her then. But she shakes him away, stands up, puts Gerda in her pocket.

Still on his knees he looks at his hands. There is blood on them where he held her wrists. "I'm sorry."

"Sorry?" she says. "Sorry!" Then she makes a kind

of song of it, a mantra. "I'm sorry. I'm sorry. I'm so sorry. So very sorry." At first her face looks soft, vacant as though she's in a trance, then her body snaps to and her eyes flash. "Did Mercy tell you something? Did she? What did she say? Mercy lies, you know. Was it about my mother? Did she speak about my mother?"

Jan hesitates.

"Do you have a problem with talking?" she shouts then. "Think it's OK just to sit and stare at people?"

He stands. "Mercy said – only that your mother was ill."

"Ill," Tilly laughs. "She never said ill. Mercy said 'sin bin', didn't she? 'Tilly's mother's in the sin bin.' That's what she said, didn't she?"

He wants to deny it, but it is the truth, so he can't.

"Well, my mother isn't in the sin bin," Tilly continues. "She's not even in detox." Her voice is rising, wobbling. "My mother's dead. She died. She's dead."

When he doesn't respond immediately (and what is he to say?), she thrusts her chin forward and adds: "You don't believe me, do you? No one believes me."

He feels his heart tick.

"I believe you," he says.

10

I watch him go down the slope, a shadow moving against the dark sky. He has a slightly loping walk, a walk bigger than he is, the walk of a man, or a wolf. I track him all the way across the field to the barred, metal gate. I watch him climb into the town, disappear.

When he leaves my horizon, it's as if he was never there. The landscape lies still and undisturbed. Did I make him up? Did I walk him up to the bridge and away again? It seems so, as I stand here alone in the semi-dark, the hairs on my arms lifting beneath my sleeves. But something remains. It's the tune. Some part of it is still in my head. I couldn't have imagined that. I didn't even know I was listening, but I must have been, even when I was cutting. A sweet, melancholy tune, but too low, as if a colour was missing. That's what I heard. Jan playing the Antara. Not as Inti would have played, swelling with carnival, with exuberant love, but as if the very next breath he took might crush his heart in his chest.

And then he kissed me. Or at least I think he kissed me. I put my hand up to my lips, touch where he touched. My lips feel full, fat, as though he sucked on them. But he did not. Just closed his mouth over mine and then – walked away. He walked away. Can you kiss someone and then walk away?

I can hear the sound of a train coming, that loud, low, rumbling. And I find myself on tiptoe, as if I'm going to run again. I'm poised and the train's coming, I can feel the wind of it, a thousand kisses against my cheek. How long is it since anyone kissed me, anyone at all? I speed to the edge of the bridge, where the brick wall begins. I must go now, if I'm going, because the train is almost upon me, bellowing at my back. But I hesitate. What if I didn't make it up? What if he did kiss me, what then? The train screams and whooshes and I flatten myself against the wall, which is lucky because the train is on the inside track.

Sixteen carriages of certain death, missing me. And then it's gone and I'm still there. Alive. Kissed.

In my pocket something stirs, moves. It's Gerda.

I pull her out. She's upside down. I right her.

"Gerda!"

Her eyes look at me. She can see! I could burst for joy. But can she speak? Can she?

"The kiss," says Gerda and she pauses. I wait with trembling delight, trembling anticipation, feel again the boy's lips on mine. "The kiss," repeats Gerda, "it never happened. You made it up."

When I get home they all talk at once. Their voices tumble on top of each other. Grandma's is the loudest, or maybe just the one I'm listening to, because I don't want to hear what Gerda's saying.

"Where have you been?" Grandma says. "I've been so worried about you. Mrs Van Day called. Why did you run out of her house like that? You've been hours. I've been going demented. I've had to tell your father. I nearly rang the police. One more hour and I would have rung the police. Have you had anything to eat? You look half-famished. Did you have any lunch? I bet you didn't have any lunch, did you? Shall I make you hot milk? Why did you do it, Tilly, put that stuff in the Van Days' food? I thought Mercy was a friend of yours? She did stand by you, you know, when... I've got everything ready for you for tomorrow. All your clothes washed and ironed. Folded. On your bed. I've done everything. Why don't you tell me what's going on? I'd like to help, Tilly. You know I would. Why do you think I came to live here in the first place? Only because of you. You know that don't you? I'd rather have stayed in my own home, the one I shared with Gerry. So many memories in that house. If only your parents hadn't divorced. History repeating itself. But at least Gerry died. Didn't walk out on me. Walk out on Judith. She was only fourteen, you know, when Gerry died. Same age as you are now. He had so much to give her and he died. Can't blame Gerry though. Can't really blame Richard. Takes two, and even though she is my daughter, Judith. Well, what can I say? And... oh what are we going to do, Tilly? If only Gerry were still here, he'd know what to do. Gerry always knew what to do. Gerry loved me. Really loved me. What about toast? Hot buttered toast, you must be able to put away some toast?"

My father screams: "And don't bother to come to the restaurant next week." Of course he doesn't really scream, because he's not even in the house. Not in person anyway. He's on the notepad by the phone, shrieking in Grandma's spidery handwriting. *Richard. Tilly. Don't come. Sunday. Got cover.* Tell her she's not needed. I've got Aaron and Billy. Responsible people. Tilly's too like Judith. Not to be trusted. It runs in the genes.

Of course the note only really says the bit about the restaurant, but I know what he means. I know what business means to him. Business split up my parents' marriage. Him being in the restaurant twenty-four hours a day, seven days a week. And her not. She helped out in the beginning, of course she did, was brilliant with the customers. And then there was that other Sunday – how many years ago now? Seven, eight? And he banned her. Just like that. No second chance. Couldn't risk it again, he said, couldn't trust her. He had a business to run, didn't she understand? Of course she understood, that's why she did the market, made a life for herself where she wasn't judged.

"He never kissed you," says Gerda. "What makes you think a boy like Jan would want to kiss you?"

"Not to be trusted," says my father.

"Toast," says Grandma, "did you say yes to toast?"

"Tilly," says my mother. "*Beloved.*"

Or I think she says "beloved" but her voice is very tiny and, beneath the babble, I can't quite hear.

"Look at the holes in me," says Gerda. "Have you seen where the pins were? Huge holes. You should never have left me there. Abandoned me. Why did you do that, leave me in the restaurant? Me. You should have taken care of me. Then it would never have happened. It's all your fault."

"It's all your fault," says my father. "You should exercise greater self-control. You'll go the way your mother went."

"Your clothes are all washed and ironed. You only have to put them in your drawers. It's not much to ask. I look after everything else. I'm making the toast anyway. But what you really need is a stew. I'll make a stew tomorrow. Put herb dumplings in it. You'd like that, wouldn't you?"

"Do you think," says Gerda, "just because I have stuffing inside, I don't feel pain?"

I go up to my mother's sewing room to get away from the noise, but the noise follows me. It shouts in my ear, they shout in my ear. My mother's treadle is silent. I sit down and paddle my feet furiously but there is no clunking, no childhood comfort, only the talking, the shouting which drums and hammers in my brain.

"It's all your fault. Fault. Fault. Fault."

I go to the Fairy Tale box then, reach for Red Riding Hood and put my hand beneath her skirts. I hit the hard, cool glass, pull out the bottle, unscrew the cap and inhale the foul, sweet stench. Then I drink. I tip back the bottle and pour the colourless liquid down my throat. It makes me want to retch. But I keep pouring. I barely give myself time to swallow. Something hard and high hits my brain. There's a spasm of nausea and then the floor comes to greet me. I'm all gratitude. Because I know, for a while, I will forget everything.

11

The fire doors can't be alarmed. There is a crack of dark between them already; one small push and they will swing open on the night. Jan gives that push, and then lets the doors *sshh* heavily closed behind him. He should not have come, though there were reasons, he had his reasons. He looks up at the sky: stars, of course, but pale and polluted by the light spilling from two floors of Oakwood Club activity. He moves across a manicured lawn, past a lit pond (with decorative stone cherub) and on towards the beckoning shadows of the copse which is all, Jan thinks, that remains of the original oak wood from which this club has cut its land and its name.

He turns a deliberate back on the club and its owner

(Mr Merrison, who is being especially cooperative in view of the new refurbishment and the long-term need to drum up more – and richer – business), and walks away from his mother, from Mrs Van Day, from Mercy and from the final Celeb Night discussions on acoustics and crudités and mirror balls.

The first trees Jan reaches are beech, tall and graceful. But they do not detain him, he is tracking inwards to where he can see the spreading shape of an ancient oak. Royal tree of England. It draws him. If he were a real Chilean boy, what would his tree be then? What bark would he press his back to in the mountains of his unknown homeland? What stars would shine for him? For the stars of the cold north are not those – or not only those – visible to southern eyes, the eyes of his mother. How can he imagine his mother if he cannot imagine her sky? Besides, it's important, because of the grandfathers. All of them, the Chileans (his grandfather, his great-grandfather, his great-great-grandfather), they are all in the heavens, looking down upon him from their starry heights. They speak to him, whisper ancestor words, know things, these grandfathers. Grandfather Haldane Lock, he is also up there, staring, starring down.

Jan arrives at the oak and stands beneath its age.

Through its branches the stars come to him. Grandfather Lock, his English mother's father, was the first person Jan ever saw in a coffin.

"Haldane, do you know what it means, lad?"

"No."

"Half-Dane. Half-Dane, half-Yorkshireman. Neither fish nor fowl, that's me lad."

And Jan had known what Grandfather Lock was talking about, and why Grandfather Lock had squeezed his eight-year-old hand. Haldane Lock never said "thee and me, both", but that's what he meant, the half-Chilean boy and the half-Danish grandfather. And then he died. There wasn't much said. A disease perhaps. Old age. Though he never seemed that old, with his undimmed blue Danish eyes. But then he was in a box, and Jan's mother wept. Jan did not weep, just went into the night and located Rigel, the star at Orion's heel (the place where the Chilean grandfathers shone) and looked. And there he was, just to the south, a bright, intermittent and previously unnoticed star. Grandfather Lock. An Englishman could not be among the stars. But a half-Dane. Yes.

His mother had caught Jan once, leaning out of a window, speaking to stars.

"What are you doing?" she'd asked.

But of course he hadn't said. It would worry her if she thought he heard them talking, and they did talk, sometimes seriously, sometimes just mumbo jumbo. But even the mumbo jumbo was good. He liked the sound of their voices, the comforting murmur of them. Occasionally the grandfathers bickered. Grandfather Lock liked a joke. He amused the Chilean grandfathers, and also irritated them. Sometimes they stayed silent for weeks in a kind of protest. But Jan didn't even mind the silence; it was not against him, for they never judged him, the grandfathers. He could say or be whoever he liked and they loved him. "You're one of us," they said. "Blood and bone."

And Violeta Veron would know this. That's why the grandfathers had chosen the constellation of Orion, clumped their souls with the gas and dust of the hunter who pursued his quarry in the northern hemisphere in the winter and spring and in the southern hemisphere in the autumn. No one would have to tell Violeta Veron this, she would know where to look in the heavens and also how to listen. For his grandfather was her father and his great-grandfather her grandfather, and so on down the spiral of time.

Mother and son chained together by blood and stars, though so many thousand miles apart. But what were miles to the stars? What were days and nights?

That was another thing. Because of the turning world, his day might be Violeta's night. It pleased Jan to be awake thinking of his Chilean mother asleep and, more than this, to be asleep when she perhaps was awake, thinking of him. Because she would think of him, wouldn't she? She must think of him. Where he was, what he was doing, if he was happy.

"Boo!" Mercedes Van Day has caught him, with his back against a tree, staring at stars.

"I wondered where you'd bunked off to." She smiles that radiant smile.

Has he absented himself again, so she should follow him again? Perhaps. She is the reason he has come tonight, after all.

"Mrs Van Day wants to go to the Club, check some last-minute details," his mother had said. "Acoustics, that sort of thing. You'd be a great help at that. Test the sound system. Would you, Jan?"

And he'd said yes, because he knew Mercy would say yes, that she'd come in case he came. And there is something Jan needs to know. It is about kissing.

122

Because Mercy does want to kiss him, he is sure of that. And he wants to kiss her, oh yes. How could he not? His whole body jangles when she is near. This is what he wants to know: can a kiss be claimed? Would you know you'd kissed Mercy in a way it is impossible to tell with Tilly? Because Tilly refuses you, won't let you in. Makes a kiss a nothing thing, something to be forgotten, something that might never have happened. And also, put more bluntly, when Mercy looks at him, Jan feels he might explode inside.

But, before he can begin, there is one thing itching his mind. "The doll," Jan says, "Tilly's doll, why did you stick pins in it?"

"What?" Mercy says and then: "Oh that. I didn't stick pins in it. Cindy did. The dressmaker." She pauses, checks his eyes. "I just had the doll on a table in the drawing room and Cindy... why... did you see Tilly, then? Did she mind?"

Jan is silent.

"OK, she minded. I'm sorry. But it wasn't intended and Tilly... she does let little things get to her."

Jan imagines a pin in the Violeta Veron doll. It would be bigger than the doll's whole body. He imagines also, or tries to, how it would be not to be affected by little things. Not to be half-Dane or half-Chilean or half anything, but to be one hundred per cent oneself. Confident and bright and smiling, like Mercedes Van Day. He imagines how it would be to love someone like that, immerse yourself in them, their boldness, their certainty, their unshakeable oneness. And just for a moment an image of the two girls comes to Jan: Tilly as a small but raging sea and, lying placid as a lake behind her, Mercedes Van Day.

"The stars," Mercy says. "Aren't they wonderful tonight?"

He follows her eyes heavenwards. She will not see her ancestors, she will not hear them buzzing in her ears. What will she see? Pinprick planets and moons, distant galaxies, things beautiful and other? He looks at her with awe. And longing. She seems so free.

"Makes you feel small," she says, "looking up. As though you were nothing."

She is standing very close to him. He can see the rise and fall of her chest as she breathes. She comes closer still, or maybe he has moved. They are both very close to the tree. But the tree can not have moved. So it must be her. Or him.

"That's what I feel," she says (that breath is on his

face now, warm and sweet), "when you play guitar. That the music's big and everything else is small. I'm small and that's all right. It doesn't matter. Because the music is so beautiful."

This astonishes him. He has not played for her. She has heard nothing. Only seen him tonight pick up a guitar because his mother asked, because Mrs Van Day asked, just to hear the Club's sound system. It wasn't even his own guitar. He strummed nothing important, did it at best unwillingly, at worst perfunctorily. Played what tune? Part of the tune from the bridge? He doesn't think so. Though maybe he lost himself for a minute or two, stopped noticing the time or the people, once his hands were on the strings. Could he have gone inside the music, given himself away? Or did she really hear something, does she know something, about him, about his longing?

"So you will play tomorrow night, won't you? You must play. It would be criminal not to."

Her head is tipped upwards, her eyes look straight into his. Her lips are slightly parted.

"Please," she says, and her back seems to arch, as though she's lifting herself towards him. "For me?"

His answer, if it is an answer, is to bend down and fasten his mouth over hers. There is no scream in this kiss, just a kind of melting. Her body (or is it his?) seems to dissolve, so he puts his hand behind her head, in the hair at the nape of her neck, as if that would support her, support them both. And they hold together and it isn't clumsy at all and she doesn't pull away, not for a long time.

12

My father says I have to go to the Celeb Night. My grandmother says I have to go. Gerda says so.

"I've paid for the sodding tickets," says my father.

"You'll enjoy it once you get there," says my grandmother.

"You have to," says Gerda, with a full stop like a slap.

When she didn't speak, she wasn't dead, Gerda tells me. Just furious. All that time I waited for her to breathe and she'd just sent me to Coventry. It never occurred to me, but it should have done, because my mother could be like that. Cut you off in the middle of a sentence. Or, at least, cut Dad off. Never me. No. She never did it to me. My mother loved me. Loves me. Gave me Gerda. But my father, there were times she wouldn't speak to him for a week. Made a wall of ice if he came in the room. Like when he hid her motorcycle helmet.

"You're not fit to be driving. You're a danger on the road," my father said.

So she sent him to Coventry for a week and drove without her helmet.

"That'll show him," she said.

And it did. He gave the helmet back.

"At least you'll be safe," he said. He always loved her. Always.

And me?

"If you don't go to that Celeb Night," says my father, shouting in the kitchen, "it'll be a waste of money. I sweat blood for that money."

"But if I go and I hate it, won't that be a waste too?"

"But not of money!" he says.

No, not of money.

"In any case," I try, "it's for charity, and they get the money whether I go or not. In fact they've got the money already, so why does it matter?"

"It matters to me. I made a deal. With Mrs Van Day.

Part of my apology on your behalf. Now you have to complete your side of the deal."

"So it's a penance!"

"Yes," says Gerda. "It's a penance."

"No," says my father, "it's a bloody expensive night out. You should be grateful."

"It will cost more to go than not to go."

"What?"

"You have to have an outfit. Dress up. That's what it is, a Celeb Night, you have to be a celebrity."

"Well, you have your mother's sewing machine. Make something! Or didn't she pass those genes on?"

The sewing room. That's where Grandma found me the night I put my hand up Red Riding Hood's skirts. Grandma scooped me up (even though she's frail and old) and put me to bed. Least I imagine Grandma did that because I could not have made my own way to my bedroom, nor got undressed, and there I was in the morning, in a fresh nightgown in my own clean bed. So clean, in fact, I wondered if Grandma had had to change the sheets in the night. But nothing was said. Not by me and certainly not by Grandma. That's not Grandma's way. But she did take away the bottle. That is Grandma's way. Not that there was much — if anything — left of the retching, wretched liquid. Of course, I went to check, put my hand back up the petticoats. Nothing. It's possible, of course, that there never was a bottle under Red Riding Hood's skirt. It's possible that I imagined the bottle, dreamed it in that nice clean bed.

"You dreamed nothing," said Gerda. "Now go to the room and make the dress."

Possible that I dreamed Jan's lips over mine out at the bridge.

"Yes," says Gerda. "That you did dream."

That's the problem with the Red Riding Hood liquid, it makes you confused. It makes you forget.

"Jan..." I begin.

"Cares nothing for you," says Gerda. "Now make the dress."

And if he had cared, he would have come, wouldn't he? He would have rung. Left some message. A whole week of silence now. And he hasn't been to the bridge, because I've been there.

So Gerda must be right.

I go upstairs to my mother's sewing room. I will make the dress.

"That's it," says Gerda. "Good girl."

Grandma's words return to me: "It will be easy when you decide who you want to be. Who do you want to be, Tilly?"

"*You are who you are,*" says my mother, "*why try to be someone else?*"

And I know then what I will do. I take my mother's sewing scissors, the Wilkinson Sword ones with the very sharp blades, and go to the linen basket in which my mother kept her remnants. I open the lid and pull out the brightly coloured entrails, the scarlet velvets, the fairy-tale blue satins, the offcuts of (fake) shocking pink snakeskin. I dig deeper, looking for the dun colours, the ugly colours: the oranges, the dirty yellows, the greys. Feel for the rougher fabrics, for my mother collected everything. "You never know," she said, "when things will come in handy." So here they are, of course, a yellowing piece of flannelette, the fraying lower leg of a pair of grey trousers, and yes, an old sheet, 60s orange. I pull out my spoils and attack them with the scissors. I cut and I hack and I tear. I know what I'm doing. I enjoy the sound of the ripping, imagine the blade that knifed through my mother's leather biking gear.

Gerda looks on, impassive.

Then I begin to sew. I don't use the treadle, partly because I don't know how to make my feet and my hands act in rhythm, and partly because what I'm doing calls for hand stitching. I thread a needle with black, sew the severed pieces of cloth back together. The stitches are large, ungainly, they look like stitches you see on corpses in films after the body has been through an autopsy. But I don't care. I try the frock on. It doesn't fit, but that doesn't matter either. So I keep cutting and I keep stitching until I am satisfied that the thing I am making is finished.

"It isn't finished," says Gerda. "There is no pocket for me."

I cut more of the orange sheet, carefully now, sew a pouch, secure it beneath the skirt.

"That's better," says Gerda.

Then I walk to my mother's bedroom, put on the garment and look at myself in my mother's full-length mirror.

Gerda, looking out from the pocket, likes what she sees. She smiles.

13

We arrive late. I am wearing the garment, a coat (which totally covers the garment) and no shoes.

Grandma says: "You can't go to a ball with no shoes."

"It's not a ball, Grandma. In any case, bare feet is what this outfit needs."

"What outfit?" says Grandma. "Who are you going as? Why don't you let me see?"

I contemplate saying, "You wouldn't understand," but actually, Grandma might understand, so I say: "You're not dressed up. You're just going as yourself."

"Oh Tilly," says Grandma. "I'm seventy-three years old. How many seventy-three-year-old pop stars do you know?"

"Not pop stars, Grandma, celebrities."

But, of course, it is not about pop stars, or even celebrities, it's about not pretending, about accepting who you are.

She looks at my feet. "I don't think there are any celebrities who go barefoot. What would the shoe industry think? Why don't you put on something, Tilly, if only to get to the car?"

And so the argument goes on, which is why we are late. Grandma takes her coat to the cloakroom, exchanges it for a white raffle ticket. I keep my coat on. Grandma sighs.

"You're as stubborn as your mother," she says. She takes my arm. "Come on."

The double doors of the Oakwood Club function room are flung wide. The event comes to greet us before we step inside: the bright spangled lights (reflected in wall-sized mirrors), the excited buzz, the low throb of disco music, the clink of glasses, the laughter. I can hear Mercy laugh. I can also smell the alcohol, as it moves on the air, sweet and warm.

"Gosh," says Grandma, "quite a turnout."

We go in. I scan the room for Jan, but I can't see him anywhere. Mercy I can see, she is standing very close to the entrance, chatting to Charlie and to a boy I don't know. She has put in blonde hair extensions and her normally trim bob is like a lion's mane. As she moves the wildcat hair swings thickly about her, lapping her back and brushing the satin curves of her breasts. Her exposed stomach is bronzed and tight and her legs shimmer beneath the blue gauze trousers. At her wrist is a large plastic disc with the number 9 written on it in permanent ink. Her number for the celebrity parade. Vote Mercedes Van Day. Vote Britney. Star. Beauty. The boy I don't know (who is wearing an England number 7 shirt and a blond mohican – Beckham) is looking at the star with hungry eyes. As Jan would, if he were here. How could he not?

I clutch the coat tighter about me. I have made a mistake. In my mother's sewing room, with Gerda beside me, it all seemed so obvious, so right. Making the garment was an act of defiance. It said, "I don't care. I'll go – but on my own terms. I'll be who I am. You won't break me. None of you. It may be a penance but I can parade that penance. I can still be strong. I will not give up. I choose my own rags, flaunt myself as the Cinderella whose prince doesn't care and whose godmother is dead." But, being here, I find I do care. I find, standing next to star and beauty, Mercedes Van Day, that I cannot take off my coat. My parade is a sham. To take off the coat would be to die of humiliation.

Britney Van Day turns around. "Hello Mrs Barker," she says to my grandmother, teeth gleaming. And then she sees me, eyes me. Up. Down.

"Mercy," says Grandma. "You look..." She pauses, observes the transparent trousers and the satin bikini bottoms beneath, "... magnificent. Who exactly are you?"

Mercy laughs. "Who exactly are you, Tilly?"

"Tilly..." Grandma begins – and then something catches her eye. It's the hand of her old friend Audrey Phillips, waving from across the room. Grandma, who thought she would know no one here tonight, says, "Oh, excuse me..." and she walks away. My grandmother abandons me.

"Let me guess," Mercy says to me, "you're Mad Mac the Flasher?"

Charlie laughs, the Beckham boy laughs.

"Go on," says Charlie. "Give us a look." Even Charlie looks beautiful. She has kohled her eyes and put tiny black plaits in her hair. She's dressed in white lace and gold jewels. The disc at her wrist shows number 3, under which she's written, in luminous pink (and in case of doubt): Jennifer Lopez.

"Give us a laugh more like," says Mercy. "Take off the coat, why don't you?"

"Do as she says," says Gerda.

At least this is what I think Gerda says, but I'm not sure because that's when the band strikes up. All eyes transfer to the podium where Mrs Van Day in an Oscar-winning sheath dress of silver lamé aggresses a microphone.

"The Johnny Zando Band!" she declares and there is another drum roll and a clash of cymbals, a hoot, a cheer and an instant round of applause. "Thank you so much," says Mrs Van Day. "Well, we've seen celebrity stars numbers one to five and in a moment I'm going to call upon numbers six to ten to come up on to the stage." More hoots and cheers. "But before that, it is my very great privilege to introduce to you the first of the very talented young musicians who are going to play for us tonight. With his own rendition of M People's smash hit *Search For the Hero*, please put your hands together for the soon-to-be-legendary Jan Spark!"

The house lights dim, there is a crescendo from

Johnny Zando and into a sudden and slightly mistimed cone of brilliant white light, a figure steps. A young man with a guitar slung around his neck and dazzled eyes. The band pauses, he is to introduce himself. He hesitates, peers out from the glare into the darkened room, waits for his eyes to adjust. He is looking for something, someone. The moment lengthens. A band member drops a drumstick, it clatters on the floor. A man laughs, to relieve tension. And still Jan stares. He will not be hurried. I watch every slow turn of his body, hold my breath for him, try not to linger on his face, on those beautiful lips.

To my right, Mercy moves, she flicks her golden hair. Jan locates her and I see him smile, strum a very soft chord. At once the band responds, grateful to begin. Jan leans into the microphone. "This is," he says looking again to where Mercy is standing, "for... for someone. She knows who she is." But the band has lost patience, they are playing over him, urging him through the introduction. He lifts his head then, puts his hands on the fretboard.

Beside me Mercy flowers, her face unfurling under the gaze of the Inca god. She is radiant. Charlie looks at her in awe. Beckham lowers his head, crushed.

"You see," says Gerda.

And I do see.

You are who you are. Small and foolish.

I take off the coat.

Normally, the feel of the strings under his fingers, the indent of them, calms Jan. But he has his fingers on the strings now and he is far from calm. He is in the wrong place, doing the wrong thing. How has he come to be here? He would like to say they bullied him, coerced him, put a gun to his head. But they did nothing, unless you count saying, very politely, "please", and "will you, Jan?" and "for me?". And he wants them to be happy, all of them: his English mother, Mrs Van Day. Mercy. He's not a person to make ructions, he keeps himself quiet, has never seen the point of making waves. And yet he finds himself now in this cone of light with fumbling fingers and a sense that something has gone terribly wrong, a truth is being denied, and it is all his fault.

He looks up one final time, over to the place where Mercy stands. He has, after all, given his word. And can it really matter? It's just a charity affair, he's not being asked to make a statement about himself, is he?

It's only a bit of fun, a fun fundraiser. He's taking it all just a little too seriously.

He has missed his cue and Johnny Zando has played on, has almost got to the chorus, to finding the key to your life, when there's a skidding crescendo and a backtrack – Johnny's starting again, playing him in again, so Jan really must press his fingers on the fretboards, strum that first chord. His eyes are used to auditorium dark now, he sees the blue satin shape of Mercy quite clearly. And also the figure beside her.

A small dark figure dressed in rags. And of course he could be dreaming (he feels himself in that strange, floating, limbo state), but there again, the figure has the right face. Can he really see the face from this distance? He can. It is the face of a Chilean Cinderella, beautiful and bereft. It is the face he has searched for all these long years, the one that's always been just out of reach, just around the next corner. Violeta Veron. She has come. She has arrived. He puts his hand in the pocket of his jeans, clutches for the Worry Doll with the face of orange paper and the skirt of baked mud. His fingers prick on the wire stub of an arm. It is real. His finger bleeds.

And of course he would walk down from the stage

and across the floor and take Violeta in his arms. But he is afraid she will disappear, as she always has before, in a curl of smoke. He will be within reach of her – stretch out his hands – and, yet again, his fingers will close around nothing. Which is why he lays aside his guitar and pulls, from under his T-shirt, the Antara pipes. He will play to her. If he plays, she will understand. She will stay awhile.

What did I expect?

That I would take off the coat and the ground would open under my feet, swallow me whole? That Mercy's howl of derision would give me an excuse to curl up and die? Is this what I planned, I hoped? Well, no one has so much as twitched, especially not Mercy. Her eyes are fixed on the stage. Mine are fixed on her. There is something wrong with her face. It no longer blooms. It's tense, screwed up, etched with anxiety. She looks ugly. Can Mercy look ugly? I'm spellbound. It's the music, I suppose, or rather the noise which used to be music. The band is colliding with itself, keyboard and drums crashing together. Johnny Zando has tried to play Jan in, twice, but he has not begun, and so the band flounders. Listening to the desperate cacophony, Mercy's face is a tight prayer: he must begin, must be again her Inca god.

Then I hear it, through the crashing, a note. Just a tiny note, a puff of breath, but I'd recognise it anywhere. The Antara. Mercy's face registers disbelief. The note comes across the room as if it were directed at me alone. I turn towards the stage. Jan has the pipes around his neck, his lips to the openings. Johnny Zando, standing now, waves the band into a jerky silence. Another note. And another. Someone coughs, embarrassed. But the notes are pure and mellow and I know the tune. It is the music of the bridge, the melody he played when I cut myself and saw the blood flow. And I feel that blood again and also hear the high, melancholy wind of the bridge. And it seems to me that it is his song but also mine. That, looking at me now, facing me across the dark, he's playing for me. Which is, of course, absurd.

"Absurd," says Gerda.

But this is what I feel.

"Lift me out," commands Gerda.

I take her from the pouch.

"Hold me."

I do as she asks, hold her in my hands.

"Against your heart," she says.

I press her there. The notes are fluent now, the tune from the bridge only deeper, more haunting. And also more lovely. Whereas before there was something missing — a tone, a colour — now there is a heartbreaking completeness.

"He doesn't love you," says Gerda.

Gerda says this because she knows this is what I'm thinking, because this is what the song says. *This is for someone. She knows who she is.* Through the rags at my breast I feel the sharp edges of the beads around Gerda's wrist.

"How could he love you?" Gerda says. The beads are like little knife pricks. And then she says: "Not even your own mother loved you."

Did I have my nail against Gerda's wrist, was I pulling at those beads? Because now they are falling, like tiny red petals on to the floor. I watch them spin, but there is no noise when they hit the carpet, just a series of tiny, tiny splashes.

And then I'm back in that room again, the place where I've tried so hard not to be all this time. My mother's room on the night that she died.

And didn't die.

I see it as if in a film. Me coming home from school, unusually jaunty, book bag slung across my back. No Grandma in the house. Wednesday, her bridge day. But too much silence nonetheless. No mother sounds. No treadling, no *Pluie d'amour*, no radio, no kitchen clatter, no tremulous call from the sofa in the living room: "Is that you, Tilly?"

Is that why I ran? Because I did run, straight up the stairs and into my mother's bedroom. Because of course she'd done it before. Or tried to. The door wasn't locked, so I guess she wanted to be found.

"Grandma says it was you who found her," my father said.

Of course, she knew what time I'd be back. Had it planned I suppose. Or maybe not, maybe it was just when the vodka ran out. Lying beside her was one Vladivar miniature and one full-sized Smirnoff bottle. Both empty.

She was kneeling by the bed. I can't have stood looking for more than a few seconds but the picture has freeze-framed in my mind. I mainly see the cut. She'd dragged the knife — the thin-bladed carving knife — across her wrist and was just staring at the wound, a kind of beatific smile on her face. The cut gaped, red-rimmed like a mouth. We both looked at the blood that ran along the edges, and also at the bright yellow buttery fat just inside the lips. The blood collected at the edge of the wound, some dribbled down her arm, some splashed on to the floor. Surprisingly little blood really, just small dots, like someone had got a brush and flicked red paint about. But I knew it was serious, because of that smile, and also because it was clear that she felt nothing.

Did I go to her, help her, bind her wrist with the clean tea towel she had so thoughtfully placed on the bed beside her? No, I did not. I thought about Grandma washing and ironing that towel. I wondered where the Savlon was. Often my mother put Savlon by the towel. No Savlon that afternoon. Just the knife, still in her right hand and me making no effort whatsoever to take it from her. She said nothing to me and I said nothing to her, not even: "How could you do it? How could you dare?" Because we'd been through all that.

"How could you do it, if you love me?"

"I do love you."

"Then you can't do it, won't do it, ever again. Promise me?"

"I promise."

Which is why, I suppose, I collected the cream candles and the incense, brought the red roses from the garden. I'm not saying I actually fetched these things, maybe I did and maybe I didn't. I just knew I needed something to fill the space inside me and these seemed like good things. Things she might have chosen herself, if she'd been in any fit state to choose.

No. That's a lie. And I do have to stop lying. I brought the candles and the roses and the cinnamon for myself, because I wanted there to be a different story, one that was beautiful and also one that I could finally bring to an end. So it was about control, I suppose, and the fact that I had none.

Grandma arrived then. I'm not at all sure what would have happened if she hadn't come back early that day. Sometimes I think I would have taken that knife and plunged it in my mother's breast myself. But maybe not. You have to have emotions for that sort of thing, and that afternoon, I was without emotion.

Grandma cleared up, of course. Drove my mother to the hospital. Spoke to whoever she spoke to, the Liaison Nurse probably, Alison, who works in A&E but is also a member of the Substance Misuse team. Alison, who knows my mother well. Anyway,

Grandma fixed it, sorted it as she always did, always has. And then she returned. Alone.

The tune is very high now, and far away. And of course I know Jan is not playing for me. I am foolish, but not that foolish. I look down at my hands. They feel tight and hot, as if they have been burned by a rope. Gerda is in pieces. Her head, her arms, her legs, pulled from her trunk. Her spine bent, her blue eyes ripped from her face.

It was me. There's a broken piece of sequin under one of my nails. I've blinded her. I've torn her limb from limb.

But then Gerda is only a doll.

Jan has never seen a condor, at least not with his own eyes, but there is one in his music. It is flying over a mountain at daybreak, wheeling, gliding, magnificent. The sun is bright and the air clear. Jan can see for miles. And of course he knows it is not Violeta Veron. How could it be? It's not even a woman and certainly not a middle-aged woman. It's a young girl. (Although of course, in the Chilean dream his mother is young, unblemished, for in dreams you never grow old.) But this girl is just the one from the bridge, Tilly.

Did he deliberately mistake her? Was he afraid to see what he actually saw? A dark and agitated creature whom he might also love? Did he want it to be his mother because his mother would love him (must love him) whereas Tilly might not? Can he have been so afraid? For it is Tilly. The clench and tumult of her, her hands pulling at something, as though she was pulling pieces out of herself. And yet this is why the song soars, because he is not just playing for the loss of his Chilean mother, or his distant homeland, or even for the theft of his blood name, he's playing for the girl and for her losses, for whatever it is that makes her claw so bitterly at her own flesh. And, whereas before, he wanted to bring this song (which he has dreamt so many times) to an end, now he would play forever, for the song is his kiss for her, one she may understand. But the song is no longer his own, it is spiralling upwards and he hears it reaching for an end. The song is going to end.

I put the dismembered pieces of Gerda into the pouch of the rag dress and pick up my coat from the floor. Around me people fidget. The novelty of the pipes is wearing off. They want more drinks, more and louder music, they want to be able to talk, laugh, isn't this what they've paid for? Jan is taking too long, his allotted time is over. He's an embarrassment, isn't he? And yet no one wants to be the first to move.

I move. I hug the walls, skirt the empty dance floor, I have to get to my grandmother. She is sitting with Audrey, her back to me. She gives a little shriek as I touch her on the shoulder.

"Tilly!" she exclaims, and then she sees my dress. "Oh – Tilly."

On stage, I hear a sudden spiral of notes and then a spinning fall, as if a stone had been thrown into a ravine. It is over.

"Grandma," I say, "I want to see my mother."

Jan lets go the pipes. They would fall to the floor, but for the plait of brightly coloured Bolivian wool which hold them about his neck. The light goes out on the stage. There is a silence and then a sudden burst of applause, a single person clapping ecstatically. Whether other people join in or not, Jan neither hears nor cares. He's looking out to where he last saw Tilly. She has disappeared.

The stage lights come back on. They are waiting for

a bow, perhaps. Jan turns for the steps. Where has she gone? His eyes are so focused on the faraway dark space which used to be her that he doesn't notice the figure hurrying towards him. They collide. Jan begins a mumbled apology.

"No," says the figure, and puts a finger to his lips.

It is his mother. Mrs Susan Spark.

"I never knew," she says. "Why didn't you say?" There are tears in her eyes. "Jan Veron."

"Where's Tilly?" he asks.

Sanctuary Ward is less than a mile from Oakwood.

"It's ridiculous to go now," whispers Grandma. She looks at her watch. "It's seven-fifteen already. Visiting hours finish at eight." As I don't believe she has ever visited my mother in the hospital, I'm not sure how she knows this or if it's true.

"Now," I say doggedly. "I have to go now."

"And you can't go in that... dress," Grandma hisses.

"Do you think anyone in that place is going to care about what I'm wearing? Anyhow, I've got my coat." I pull it on.

Audrey Phillips, who is sitting with her back to us, apparently engrossed in conversation with someone else, turns around then. At once Grandma rises, she nods towards her friend.

"Tilly's not feeling too good," she says in a normal voice. "We need to go home. I hope you'll excuse me."

"Oh – I'm so sorry," says Audrey.

I look Audrey in the eye and smile robustly. Grandma hurries then. We exchange the white raffle ticket for her coat and make our way to the car.

"This really isn't wise," Grandma says.

I know exactly where the hospital is, although I've never been inside. I've stood in the car park though, looking up, wondering which window was hers. I've also watched people going in and out of the front door, tried to guess which are the staff and which the heroin addicts. It's not as easy as you'd think.

"Just drive," I say to Grandma.

"There's no need to be rude," she says.

But she does drive. The rest of the journey we spend in silence. She pulls up in Raglan Road, four streets away from the hospital.

"Take me to the car park," I say. "The hospital's got a car park."

"You can walk, you've plenty of time," Grandma says.

"No," I say. "Take me to the car park. Drive in."

"No," she says.

"Why? Why not!"

"It's not raining, is it?" she says.

"No, it's not raining. But that's not the point is it?"

"I don't know what you're talking about," says Grandma.

"The point is my mother – your daughter – is a drunk. An alcoholic."

Grandma actually puts her hands over her ears, as if this information is a shock, as if this is the first time anyone has let her in on the secret.

"And you think," I continue, "that if you don't actually look, if you don't actually drive to the hospital and park in the car park, that it isn't really happening. That your daughter isn't really in there with a bunch of other drunks and smackheads." The anger is suddenly going up my throat like sick. "Just like you think if you don't actually drive me right to the school gate, then no one will know my mother's in the sin bin. Again. But they do know. They all know!"

"There's no need to shout, Tilly."

But I am shouting. "Drive me," I shout.

She doesn't respond.

"Do you think if Grandad was alive—"

"Don't pull Gerry into this."

But I pull him in: "Do you think Grandad Gerry

would have swept it all under the carpet all these years? Refused to talk about it. Refused to act? Just cleared up, cleaned up, shut up?"

"You know nothing about Gerry."

"I know everything about Gerry. You've been telling me for fourteen years. Gerry was a good man. A caring man. A decent man. Gerry had morals."

"Gerry loved me. Really loved me."

"Course he did. Well, lucky you. Lucky, lucky you!"

"On the night he died—"

"Gran, I know. On the night he died, he had more Tupperware receipts in his pocket than all the other salesmen put together."

"On the night he died—" says Grandma.

"Drive, Grandma."

"On the night he died—"

"Yeah, yeah. He had so many receipts he still got Salesman of the Week, even though he died on a Thursday. Now drive. Do what a decent man would have done, what Grandad would have done, go to the hospital. Face up to it, Gran."

Grandma puts the key in the ignition, starts the engine.

"That night—"

"I know!"

She slips the brake. "You don't know."

And there's something in her tone of voice that finally shuts me up.

"The night he died he wasn't alone." Grandma pauses. "She was with him."

"What?"

This is not the right story, the story is that Grandad Gerry wrapped his car round a tree on the long road home to Grandma, when he was driving – alone – the two hundred loyal miles back to his wife. The story is the steering column broke. And you can't tell when a steering column is going to break. So whatever happened it wasn't his fault, not his fault at all. Grandpa Gerry was blameless.

I look at Grandma, but she is staring straight ahead, watching the traffic through the car windscreen.

"Sylvia Burnley. I only found out her name at the inquest. She came of course, in person, in her high-heeled shoes. He was killed and she wasn't even scratched. There's consideration for you. Gerry all over. She cried in court. Cried and cried. Like she owned him. The affair had been going on for eighteen months. She was wearing an engagement ring."

I am stupefied. I focus on a red car in front of us,

on its particularly shiny bumper. It takes me two roads to articulate this question: "Does Mum know?"

"Of course not."

Grandma turns into the hospital car park. "And there weren't any Tupperware receipts in his pockets that day. There was an empty bottle of whisky. He was drunk, Tilly. Blind drunk."

She reverses into a parking space, brakes and then continues to stare straight ahead.

When do they hand out the books that tell you what emotion you're supposed to be feeling at any given time? I don't think I can have been in school that day. I'm sure I should feel sorry for my grandmother, extend some sort of hand to her. But my hands are folded in my lap, and I have only one thought in my head and it is this: that all those years my mother lived in the shadow of a perfect parent and a perfect marriage, which weren't perfect at all.

I get out of the car. "Thanks," I say. "Are you coming in?"

In response Grandma slumps over the steering wheel and begins to sob.

I stand there for maybe thirty seconds and then I shut the door and walk away.

*　*　*

The building is Victorian, two-storey, and has coloured tissue paper in the downstairs windows as though it were a slightly dilapidated nursery school. There is a glass entrance porch with a bell labelled "Please ring for attention". If only it were so simple.

I ring anyway and am buzzed in as far as Reception. A woman asks my business.

"I've come to see Judith Weaver. On Sanctuary Ward."

The woman observes my mac and my bare feet but says only: "And you are?"

"Tilly Weaver, her daughter."

The woman nods. Maybe there is nothing they have not already seen in here. "Sanctuary's upstairs."

I thank her and ascend the cream painted stairway with the chocolate brown carpet. The stairs twist past a window which looks out over a garden where four institutionally beige bucket chairs sit joined together, small pools of rainwater in their seats. At the top of the stairway is a glass door with a coded keypad for entry. I stand and wait at the shut door. Surely the Reception woman will have buzzed ahead? Through the glass I can see, directly ahead of me, what looks like an office and, slightly to the right, an open door labelled "Day Room". I don't like to knock, but I don't like just standing here either. A woman comes out of the office with a busy look on her face, sees me, backtracks and opens the door.

"Yes?" she says. In her hand are pills.

"I'm Tilly Weaver, Judith Weaver's daughter."

"Oh," says the woman, and she waves me in. She also looks at my feet but says nothing. She's not wearing a uniform, in fact she's dressed in a denim skirt and multicoloured cardigan, but her name label reads: "Marcia Wells, Staff Nurse".

The corridor is dark, the feel of the place small and cramped, what space there is blocked by a stack of commercial-sized plastic tubs of water. They are called Nature Springs and are still in their Cellophane.

"Are you on the list?" asks Marcia.

"What list?"

"Patients have to nominate visitors. In advance. Five only."

And would my mother have nominated me? I can't answer that question.

"Wait here," says Marcia. "I have to deal with something. I'll be back in a minute." She disappears down the dark corridor with the pills.

I edge towards the Day Room. Will my mother be there? The room is a cross between a doctor's waiting room and student sitting room. The chairs are lined up against the walls, a TV blares. There's an uneven stack of videos, a pile of magazines, a plate of biscuits. Screwed to the walls, slightly too low, are pictures, some yellow flowers, a foreign coastline.

Five people are in the room, none of them talk, or look at each other. One, a young man in his twenties, is sleeping, curled up on his own arm. He looks peaceful. An older man, immaculately dressed in black jeans and a well ironed shirt, sits astride his chair, back to the TV, looking out on to the road. Perhaps he's watching Grandma sob. I wonder then who his Grandma is, who washes his clothes and keeps him clean? A bigger, more thickset man stares at the television. He's smoking and the cigarette and his right leg wobble. He coughs and clears his throat. The other two patients are women. A young blonde, also smoking, and a woman in her thirties with black hair scraped into a neat ponytail, reading a book. There is nothing extraordinary about any of them, and that gives me a strange comfort. If this is a humdrum thing, if it could happen to anyone, then my mother is not a freak. I am not a freak.

I wait. The television makes a joke.

No one laughs.

A clock ticks.

Tick. Tick.

Where are you, Mama?

"Oh Matilda, it is Matilda Weaver, is it?"

"Yes."

Marcia is back with a list. "Come with me." She leads me to the office, the door is wedged permanently open with a bottle of Nature Springs. "You are on the list."

This fact makes me feel suddenly tearful. Did my mother put me on the list before – those times I didn't visit?

"But I'm afraid I'm going to have to search you," Marcia says. "You do understand, don't you?"

And I suppose I do.

"Lift your arms, please." I lift them. What are friends and family for if not to bring you comfort, the smooth glass comfort of a miniature, a reeling little bottle of Vladivar?

"And turn out your pockets."

In my mac pockets are a Tazo disc from a cereal packet, a bus ticket, a dirty tissue and a twenty pence piece.

Marcia smiles wanly, gestures at me to put them away. "Now just take off your coat, please."

I take if off. Now even Marcia cannot keep the surprise from her face.

"Just been to a fancy dress party," I inform her.

"Has it got pockets?" she asks.

"No. I mean yes."

She nods.

I turn out the pouch. Show Marcia Gerda's severed legs, her arms, her face with the gouged-out eyes.

"Was it a voodoo party?" asks Marcia.

"No," I say, and then I make a speech. "And anyway people have the wrong idea about voodoo. The word 'voodoo' actually comes from 'vo' meaning 'introspection' and 'du' meaning 'into the unknown'. And it's not about dolls so much as about 'loa', the spirits, spirits of the ancestors mainly."

"Right," says Marcia. "Is that what they teach you in school these days?" She feels into the corners of the pouch, brings out a half-sequin. "OK," she says. "Thank you for that. And I'm sorry, but it's the rules."

I put the pieces of Gerda away.

"Your mother's in Room Five, second on the right."

The door to Room Five turns out to be labelled DF16. It's the sort of door you might find in a pretty jail. Blank, but with a window, the bars of which are in fact the crisscross grill of patterned safety glass. Behind the glass is a small, floaty, summer-flower curtain and above it is a slot for a name, only there is no name. What might she have put there? Judith, Mrs Weaver, Mother, Mama, Big? Perhaps there is no name because when you come in here you lose your right to a name, or maybe it's just that by the time you get here you have no idea who you are any more.

I knock and enter without waiting for permission. The room is in fact only half a room, a chipboard wall dividing what must once have been an elegant first-floor bedroom. The effect is to make the half-room too thin and the wrong shape, the once graceful bay window cleaved in two and banged up against the chipboard wall. The furniture is cheerless: a rickety chair, a hospital bed, a wardrobe, a small set of – lockable – drawers. On the bed, staring at the ceiling, lies Mama, my mother. Big.

Only she doesn't look big at all. In fact, in the moment before she rolls over and sees me, it occurs to me that she's the smallest person I've ever seen in my life. She's lying very still and has her arms crossed over her breast, her hands on her shoulders, as if she is trying to hug herself. Her feet (like mine) are bare, tiny, of course, and, against the black of her trousers, seem an unearthly white. It's not cold in the room but I know those feet will be cold. I have an instinctive desire to cover them up. Her wounded wrist is concealed, flush against her black T-shirt. And I can see nothing of her blue eyes, fixed as they are on the ceiling, but it's still as much as I can do to stop myself launching my body at the bed, flinging my arms around her. She turns then.

"Matilda," she says, "is that you Matilda?"

"Yes."

She heaves her huge body to an upright. And yes, actually, it is a big body, massive and fleshy, but so hunched and curled over, there might be nothing inside at all.

"Really you? Let me touch you." She stretches out an arm and then withdraws it quickly. "Because there have been ants. And earwigs. They came in my left ear and ate their way through my brain. Or least that's what I dreamed. Come." She stretches towards me again.

I move closer, I go into her touch.

She takes my hand in hers, squeezes it tighter than bearing. I see the cut. It's healed into an ugly red welt, the lower edge weeping a little clear liquid. There are marks where stitches have been. And I know most hospitals use SteriStrips now, so I wonder if they have done this to punish her.

"Why didn't you come before?" she asks. "Why do you never come? Why do you leave me here?" Her voice sounds so like Gerda's. "Have you any idea what they do to you in here? They withhold your medication. I'm supposed to have medication four times a day. But they've cut it down to three. Two. They say they have it controlled, under control. But they're not the ones lying here, sweating. Do you know how much I sweat? Sometimes my back is drenched. Drenched. And my hairline, my forehead. They said it would go, stop after just a few days. A few days! And the shaking. And you can't sleep. I haven't slept a wink since I came here. Not an hour, not a minute. But I dream. Oh yes I dream, do you know what I dream, Tilly? I dream that the nurses are eating me up, that they eat me up, starting with my feet. Can you imagine what it's like having those people who should be caring for you eating you up?"

"Yes," I say, "I can imagine."

Then I make myself remember. I walk myself around our house on the days that Grandma cleared away the vodka and my mother prowled for cough medicine, for aftershave, for things under the kitchen sink, anything anaesthetic to throw down her throat. I watch from the doorway again, recalling the days when she could barely stand, when she held on to a chair and practised in front of a mirror how to hand over cash before she took that trip to the off-licence. I hear her slurred voice: "A bottle of Shmirnoff, pleesh," listen to the pathetic noise of her fingers scrabbling inside her purse for cash. I walk myself from the sitting room, smelling the vomit, to the bathroom, smelling the vomit, to her bedside, smelling the vomit.

"You're not listening," my mother says.

"I'm listening," I say.

"You do love me don't you, Tilly? Because I don't know what I'd do without you."

A silence.

"I love you Tilly, you do know that, don't you?"

"Yes."

"So you do love me?"

"Yes," I say. "I love you, Mama."

15

It is ten minutes since Jan arrived in the car park, maybe a quarter of an hour. He's waiting in the grainy dark, a spit of rain in the air. He would wait all night, but this may be the wrong place, she might not be here at all.

He scans the lit windows of the Victorian building. Only one window is uncurtained, a bay on the upper storey. A man, sitting behind the glass, stares out. He hasn't moved since Jan arrived. But then Jan hasn't moved much either, just stood in his T-shirt, Mercy's words ringing in his ears: "Did your Cinderella turn into a pumpkin?"

Perhaps it had been rude of him to descend upon Mercy (directly from the stage) and, quite forgetting to mention her captivating outfit of blue gauze, say: "Where is she, where's Tilly, where has she gone?" But then it was Mercy whom Tilly had been standing beside.

"How should I know?" Mercy had said, and then: "Didn't she leave a glass slipper?"

The anger was quite unmistakable, quite unmasked and it would have been nothing for him to backtrack, observe the courtesies. For hadn't he said: "This is for someone – she knows who she is"? And of course Mercy might reasonably have thought he meant her (and perhaps he did – even though the dark figure beside her was so very close and quite in view). But he wasn't quick enough to say anything at all before Mercy spoke again: "What are those pipe things anyway?"

"Antara," he'd said. "From Bolivia. In winter you have to put seeds in them. Pulses. Just a few. Or they play too low. Where is she?" he couldn't help adding as he touched the pipes and heard the tiniest rattle of those seeds. "Where's Tilly?"

It was Charlie who spoke up. She'd overheard some remark made by Audrey Phillips, who was (apparently) a friend of Tilly's grandma's.

"Well, if she's gone to see her mother," said Mercy, her smile as tight as a cat's, "then she'll have gone to the sin bin."

And of course he'd had to ask for the address and of course Mercy had said she'd be delighted to supply it, after all there was only one state-funded place for pissheads in town, and, she intimated, Jan's concern was touching.

So here he was in the car park of the hospital, trying once again to stop a dream spiralling away into just so much smoke.

His mother had offered to drive him, of course, but he'd refused. It was only a mile, he'd said, and he needed the walk. Actually he needed to be alone. To sort something out in his brain. Because once again Tilly had fled, hadn't she? He'd played her the tune, the one he thought she'd understand above all others and she'd simply run away. He wanted to walk the mile to acknowledge the madness of coming after her yet again. Well, he'd acknowledged it and here he was. Waiting.

There was someone else waiting, he noticed. An old woman in a car. When he'd arrived she'd been crying, the sobs violent enough to rock the whole of her slight body. Her head banging, at one point, against the glass of the driver's window. But the crying had ceased. The old woman had blown her nose and was now sitting erect, waiting.

Waiting.

And now the door to the glass porch opens and he (and the old woman in the car) both turn expectantly. But it is not Tilly. Just a man in a light jacket with the collar turned up. And Jan is about to look away again, begin the wait again, when, from behind the man, a smaller figure emerges. It is her. He knows it from the tilt of her head and also from the tight feeling in his chest.

"Tilly!" he wants to call. But he does not. He merely remains standing where he's been standing all this while. In the shadows. For somehow he hasn't quite got imaginatively beyond this point, the point at which she emerges and he – does what? Says what? Says what, mainly. It's while he's standing there, all the words in his mouth swallowed down, that Tilly sees him.

"You," she says. There is no surprise whatsoever in her voice.

He stands and stands.

"So now you know," she says. "I lied. My mother isn't dead at all. She's in the sin bin. Just like Mercy always said."

And now he does speak, grabs her by the wrists (in case she thinks to run again) and it all starts spilling out of him, and he doesn't know if the words are in the right order, but maybe that doesn't matter, because surely she can feel the heat in him as he speaks about perfect mothers who aren't really perfect at all. "You see," he tells her, "I have a mother who is dead and not dead. Perfect and not perfect. A Chilean princess, dressed in rags, who never grows old, never will grow old, who gave birth to me, held me, loved me, loved me so much she knew she must give me up, because she was dirt poor, starvation poor, and if I was to die, how could she bear that? How could any mother bear that, when there was another way, another mother standing by with open arms?"

Tilly looks quite bemused, shocked even, and it occurs to Jan that he's going too fast and hasn't even mentioned the word "adopted", hasn't actually said it, "I'm adopted", but she isn't pulling away, so Jan takes a chance and dips one hand in his pocket to bring out the Violeta doll. He opens his palm so she will see the wired thing with the sand and tarmac hair and the skirt the colour of baked mud; pushes beneath her face the arm that's only a rusted stump, the one that was never quite long enough to hold him.

"And of course that was love, she loved me," he says, because he's been saying it to himself for so many years (and so has his English mother). "To give away your own child, what greater love could there be?" And then he stops, because he knows what a dangerous brink he's on.

So it's Tilly who has to jump. "Or maybe the greater love," Tilly says in a voice that sounds quite faraway, "would have been to keep you. Keep you close whatever, forever."

And now he really can't speak. His throat is closed up. Not least because the girl is crying, though her tears fall without any noise at all. He puts a hand up to touch one of those tears, tastes it, wet and salty. He has never been able to cry about this himself.

She puts a very soft finger on his lips then.

"Did you kiss me?" she asks. "Up at the bridge. Did you kiss me?"

He nods, feels the finger move on his mouth.

But still she waits, it's almost as if she's listening for

another voice, for someone to disagree, to say there was no such kiss. But there is only the night wind about them.

She leans upwards then, places her mouth against his and kisses him with an urgency which is almost famished. There is nothing in his life which has prepared him for this.

And who knows how long they might have held that kiss but for the sharp honk of a car horn?

Honk. Honk. Honk.

Tilly pulls away.

"Grandma," she says and she touches her lips with her hand.

It's the old lady in the car.

"She was crying," Jan says.

"I know," says Tilly. "Which is why I ought to go."

And she walks away. But, for the first time, Jan knows she is not leaving. She turns, halfway towards the car, and she looks at him. But he knows anyway, this just confirms it. If he were a winged creature, he would fly around the world this night. He would take off and circle the planet. Twice. Three times. He'd flip round Orion, say "hi" to the grandfathers and return to earth barely out of breath. Tilly is not a dream, not a puff of smoke, Tilly exists. Real as a mountain.

As Tilly's car leaves the car park, a white Rover drives in. He recognises it at once. Susan Spark. She takes the space vacated by Tilly's grandmother. She can see him of course, he's standing in her headlights. She switches off the engine but she doesn't get out. Waits for him to make the first move, afraid of course that she's interfering, because she's come when he said, quite categorically, "I want to walk." Want to be alone. But suddenly he feels quite exhausted. There is no one he could be more grateful to see.

He walks to the car and gets into the passenger seat.

Her face is all concern, but she still waits for him to begin.

"Thank you," he says.

And she smiles like he's given her a gift.

"Do you want to go home?"

He nods.

She starts the engine again, slides them silently into the night. She asks him nothing else, just keeps her peace and his. Then his love for her, which has been so quiet and so constant down all the years, flows over him. He wants so much to say something to acknowledge her place in his life, to make her understand how much her soundless intimacy means to him. But perhaps she knows already.

And so they travel together, gently, until (maybe aware of his noiseless need) she finally relinquishes, and says: "Is everything all right?"

And he replies: "Yes."

He remembers her face at the Oakwood Club, a bright face lit with tenderness but also with fear, how she said: "I never knew" and then used his name, spoke it to him the first ever time: "Jan Veron." Said it as if it contained a loss, as if being Veron he could not be Spark. But watching her there beside him, he knows he is also Spark. He is also for her as she has been for him. Susan Spark with arms not of rusted wire but of flesh and blood. Arms which have ached from holding him.

"Yes," he says, "everything is all right." And then he adds, "Mum."

76

The pyre is Jan's idea. He says we should take the dolls and go to the bridge, so we do. Our mothers, he believes, are like a grief only there's never been a funeral. He wants us to make a funeral, a celebration and a mourning.

He brings matches and a penknife, but everything else, he says, we will find. The last few days have been dry but I still think it will be damp up at the bridge.

"It will be all right," says Jan.

It is strange and soothing to walk with him to the railway line. Previously we have both made our way here alone. Yet we walk in each other's prints, as though my path was always his and his mine. I remember how he loped away like a wolf the time of that first kiss, and now that stride is beside me, velvety, powerful.

When we reach the brow of the railway hill, he pauses, scans the wild horizon.

"The elderflower," I say.

"Yes," he says. "Of course. You know, then."

"Know what?" I have selected the elderflower only because of its position, because in an undergrowth which can be dense, this stunted tree has claimed some ground for itself, has a little space around it. And maybe — perhaps — because this is the place where I sank that day I tried to breathe life into Gerda.

"The Celts," says Jan, "thought the elder could cure mankind's ills. They used the wood for pyres, put elder twigs into coffins, planted pieces in the earth around a grave. They believed wherever the elder grew, that was a sacred place, one that could not be despoiled."

"How do you know that?"

"You knew it," he says, "before I said a thing. You chose that tree."

And I'm about to protest when I see there are other spaces, other trees, amongst the undergrowth that I might have chosen, might have sunk against — but didn't.

"You can understand with your heart," says Jan, "as well as your eyes. Must understand. Else what's the point?"

Beneath the tree is a low-lying carpet of green.

Moss and fern-like weeds, dock leaves and that loose, stringy, sticky plant that winds itself about your ankles, clings to your clothes. There are also nettles.

"Watch out!" I say to Jan as he begins to clear a space.

"They're not stingers," he says. "They're White Dead Nettles. You can suck the flowers. They taste of honey."

"How long since you've been coming here?"

"A few years. Forever."

Beneath the green are thin white plant stems, dry as bones.

"Will they burn?" I ask.

"Not well enough."

I go hunting for more substantial kindling. I find a fallen log, too big and too damp, but also a dead tree, with branches dry enough to snap. I take what twigs I can break easily and then, further on, beyond the broken concrete posts and the sheet of corrugated iron, I spot a packing case.

"Perfect," Jan says when I return to him. He has cleared and levelled a small oval of earth. He gets out his knife and strips the thinner wood from the sides of the crate.

I make myself watch the flash of the blade, pay attention to how calm I am. Just a knife blade, just stripping an old fruit crate. Jan feels my eyes, stops what he's doing.

"Did it hurt when you cut yourself?" he asks.

"No."

"And when your mother cut herself?"

"Yes. Of course."

He nods, puts away the knife and begins to build the fire. He interlocks an airy tower of black sticks and white pieces of packing crate.

"Do you want to cut a piece of the elder?" he asks.

"OK."

"You have to ask permission."

"What?"

"Ask permission. Of the tree."

I look to see if he's serious. He's serious. I imagine how it would be if anyone but Jan asked me to talk to a tree. But then no one has been – or could be – Jan.

"The ancient foresters," he says, "wouldn't even touch an elder without asking, let alone cut it. They were afraid of the Elder Mother."

I am afraid of the knife. But I ask for it.

"Can I borrow the knife?"

He hands it to me. I flip open the blade, hold it close to a branch that seems dead.

"No," says Jan, "you must take a living piece."

"It won't burn," I say.

"True."

I move in a branch, take a small, flexible, sappy piece of wood between my finger and thumb. The penknife blade is bright.

"Elder Mother, I ask permission to take a piece of your living tree for the pyre of the mothers who were dead but who now live, who were perfect but who are now imperfect."

There's a pause.

"How do I know if she's given permission?"

"You don't. You have to take the risk."

That's when I know I'm going to giggle. It breaks over me, a great, waving, convulsing giggle. And I can't stop it, but I can muffle it. I clap my hand over my mouth, for fear of offending the moment, offending Jan. But he's smiling.

"That's the first time I've heard you laugh," he says.

I stop laughing.

"Tilly..." he says. And I know he's going to kiss me. But he pauses, of course, and the waiting is a hammering of sparks on my spine. In his own time, he puts his mouth on mine and his hand over my hand. We kiss and cut the branch together.

"You didn't ask permission," I say, pulling away.

Why do I always have to pull away?

"Of the elder?" he asks.

"No," I say, suddenly reckless. "Of me. For the kiss."

"You have to take the risk," he says.

If I hadn't loved him before I think I would do now.

"Or of the elder," I say.

"You asked for both of us. Anyway, this is a funeral. Have some respect."

And then we both laugh and I think I've never felt so comfortable with another human being as I do with him.

"Knife."

And I haven't even realised I still have the knife in my hand. The knife is a nothing. I give it to him. He cuts the elder into a piece about the size of his thumb and positions it on a strip of packing crate right in the middle of the pyre.

A train goes past then. I see it in his eyes before I hear it. We turn together, we both need to know which track it will be on, though we are both quite safe today. It's making the whining noise, the moan of the circular saw, but also the plush sound. A twelve-coach passenger train. It speeds past us on the inside track. A killer train. We watch in silence as its smoking tail disappears over the horizon.

"Why did you do it?" Jan asks then. "Why did you run that day?"

"Because... because nothing seemed that important any more, I suppose." He looks at me, waits, so I add: "It was the day after... she did it. And I think I'd just stopped caring. And also, maybe, some part of me wanted to feel what she felt. Wanted to know what it would be like to put your life in the balance. Will I die, or won't I?"

Again he nods.

"And because she asked me to come here. Gerda." From beneath my jacket I take the pouch which contains the dismembered parts of my once beloved. I lay her out on the earth beside the pyre, reassemble her, fit her arms and legs back on to their wires, place her head so close to her trunk that she might be whole again. But she isn't whole. She's missing her eyes.

"My mother made dolls," I tell Jan. "Did it for a living. But she never once made me a doll. Not even when I was a baby."

"Until Gerda," Jan says.

"No," I say. "She didn't make Gerda. I did that."

He expels a short breath, which at first I think is surprise, but then I think, no, it's realisation, as if this information suddenly makes plain something that's been troubling him. But I don't stop to enquire, because I want to say it now, want to tell him.

"The night my mother died..." I continue, then I pause, have to rephrase my mind, "... the night she made the suicide attempt, I went back to her room. Gran had left, gone to A&E. She'd asked me specifically not to return to the room, told me to go to bed. But how could I go to bed? I went back, took the knife, which was just lying on the floor, the Sabatier carving knife with my mother's blood on it, and I slashed her clothes. Put the point of the knife through every single dress my mother owned. I ribboned them. I kept thinking how they'd write it in the papers, 'It was a frenzied attack'. Pathetic. Laughable. Only I wasn't laughing.

"Then I came to her leathers. At first I didn't think I could cut those. They were like her second skin, the biking leathers. But the point of the knife was so sharp, and I put it through, I dragged it down the thigh of her trousers. It felt like killing and it made me feel good, so I did it again and again and again. I don't sweat a lot, but I was sweating. Not just angry any more but excited. It frightened me.

"And I knew I needed to calm down, needed something to focus on, something difficult to make me concentrate. It came to me like a vision. Make a doll, make the doll she never made you. And I've never been very good at sewing, but it became so obvious. I found the kid gloves in a drawer. They were the only things I took from the drawers. They had been my mother's hands when she came to kiss me goodnight, in those long-ago days when she didn't smell of alcohol. I made them Gerda's hands, her arms, her legs, her face. Then I sewed the black leather on to the white with black thread. How would my mother have done it? Would she have used white thread? Black? The stitches were ugly, but I didn't really care. I pretended that my mother was ill. That she'd died of an illness. So, of course her hands would have been feeble, the stitching poor.

"But the doll's left wrist, where the wound was. I kept seeing it. On the white white kid, I kept seeing the blood, I couldn't make it go away. That's why I assembled the bracelet, to cover it up, so I couldn't see. But, of course, I could see. The beads were red. I chose them. Red. So I could always see. Sharp red blood pricks all round her wrist. But she was as ready as she would ever be. Gerda the talisman. Gerda the mother who loved me. Who couldn't have tried to commit suicide, because you can't love someone and think to die on them."

"And the doll – Gerda – she spoke to you?"

"I spoke to me. I heard her voice. My mother's voice. And she was good, to begin with she was good. She loved me, Gerda. I made her love me, care for me, be on my side. I made her the mother I wanted, needed. I want to say deserved. But I suppose I never deserved a good mother, does anyone deserve a good mother, Jan?"

"Yes," says Jan. "Yes."

"But she turned. Gerda turned. It was like I didn't control her, even in my own mind. She started saying real things, the sort of blaming, difficult things my mother would have said... does say. Even my own doll stopped loving me."

"Put her on the pyre," says Jan.

"But the sticks are too far apart," I cry, "she'll fall through!"

"Put her on," says Jan.

"You know," I say, "the time I went to her, my mother, after Celeb Night, do you know what I was going to say? I was going to say 'No! Stop! Be quiet!' I'd torn Gerda limb from limb and I was going to do it to her. Make her understand. And do you know what I actually said? I said 'I love you'."

He looks at my face, shrugs. He knows.

He knows!

"Don't you think we should light the pyre first," I say after a pause, "before we put on... the bodies? I mean, it might not catch."

"Yes," he says. "OK." From his pocket he produces two boxes, a matchbox and a tiny brightly painted box of woven wood.

"Can I see?"

He passes me the woven box. Inside is the doll he showed me briefly at the hospital. It's tiny, only half a thumb high with a face of orange paper and a left arm that's just a broken piece of wire.

"Did your mother give you this?"

"No," he says. "Though I used to pretend that she did. Violeta Veron, my Chilean birth mother. I pretended that when she gave me away she packed with me some things to protect me, some things for me to know her by. A cut coin, of which she kept one half, a blanket she'd stitched herself, a doll. But actually I came with an institutional nightie and a pair of bootees. I used to imagine Violeta knitting the bootees. They're pale green, with a piece of blue wool around the ankle, to tie them with. But actually I think they came from the organisation that effected the adoption. Someone else's cast-offs."

"And the doll?"

"Mum gave me that. Part of a set of Worry Dolls. You can get them in any high-street ethnic store. I'm not saying I wasn't grateful. I was. Mum respecting my past, my roots, even though the dolls actually come from Guatemala. When I looked at them, and there were seven of them, they were all brightly coloured except this one. All made of matchwood except Violeta. And all of them had perfectly normal arms, except her. Except the mother who gave up holding me."

"She's too small to burn," I say.

He takes her from me. "I want to start again," he says. "I want to accept that I may look but I will never find her."

He lights a match, puts it to a wafer of packing case. The strip blackens and smokes. He lights another and another. One of the dead sticks catches, but there is still only smoulder. Jan bends down and blows softly. In his breath the first flame comes, intense and vivid orange. He sits back. The fire will burn.

He unknots and unwinds the paltry piece of yellow thread that does for Violeta's breast covering.

"This," he says, "is for the mother who gave me birth and whose blood runs in my veins." He drops the thread into the fire. It catches immediately, a wisp of sudden soot.

I have not thought what to say, but the words come easily.

"This is for Big." I drop Gerda's trunk into the fire. "For the mother who was always larger than life, the woman who filled my universe." The velvet bodice smokes and the plastic around the protruding wires melts and stinks.

Jan unwraps the tiny piece of dun-coloured cloth that is Violeta's dress. "This is for the mother who thinks of me in the night or who never thinks of me at all." The cloth, borne on the faintest gust of wind, falls through the lit arc of sticks to land beside the green piece of elder, where it rests and waits to burn.

I take Gerda's arms. "This is for Small. For the mother I saw at Sanctuary. For whatever the empty space inside her is." The arms fall and burn separately.

Jan slips a nail behind Violeta's head and peels the paper face from her wire body. Small bits of tarmac hair stick to her forehead.

"This is for the mother who loved me enough to give me to Susan Spark but who didn't love me enough to keep me." He puts the paper face, which has no mouth, so close to the flame that he burns his hand, but if it pains him, he says nothing.

"This is for the mother I love." I drop on Gerda's biking-leather legs. There is a faint whiff of burning flesh.

Jan untwists Violeta's wire legs from her arms. "For the mother I love."

The pieces of wire fall untouched on to the ash.

Jan has only the stump arm of Violeta left. And I have only Gerda's blinded face. Together we suspend these last things over the fire.

"And," we say together, "for the mother I..." And I know what he's going to say and I say it with him.

"For the mother I hate."

17

Jan sits beside her in silence. The fire, which was never a great conflagration, has begun to sputter and die. But there is a warmth in just being near Tilly, in knowing that, for the moment at least, she is not going anywhere. He feels cleansed by the burning, tranquil. But Tilly is edgy still, she's fiddling with a stick, peeling back its thin grey bark to reveal white, sappy innards. She rubs her fingers on the wet.

"She was drunk," Tilly says, "the day she went to register me. I was six weeks old. She couldn't remember what they'd agreed to call me. So she told the registrar, just put M. Tilly M. Weaver."

He absorbs this information slowly. Wants to tell her about Veron, how he had twice his mother's name and they still stole it from him. But when he says "Veron" to himself, even in his mind, he finds himself less angry. Because of his mother, Susan Spark, how she came to him with her gift, said: "I never knew," and then returned his name to him, "Jan Veron." And he realises, sitting up at the bridge, that he could now be Jan Veron-Spark, that this is the door his mother has left open. But will he walk through now that the choice is his? Perhaps not. Perhaps he will chose to remain Spark, elect to be Susan Spark's son? He turns the idea around in his mind.

"You're lucky," he says softly. "Can make yourself lucky. You can take a name of your own choosing." And he does tell her about Veron and as he talks he remembers reading about a tribe of Aboriginal Australians who constantly rename themselves as they change and develop through life. "They don't believe," he tells Tilly, "that any name, given you at birth, could be adequate to all things you might dream or be. So, after many years of composing music around the camp fire, a tribesman might announce, 'Now I have become Great Singer of Songs.' And the tribe welcome and honour and use that name. So take a name, Tilly, create yourself anew."

And who am I now? he thinks in her silence. How do I dream myself today? Juan Veron? Jan Spark? Jan Veron-Spark? Player of Pipes? Seeker of Stars? Dreamer of Dreams? Then it comes to him, sitting by Tilly and the dampening fire, and it's just one word: happy.

"Make-Believe," says Tilly. "That's what they called me. What Mercy called me."

"Forget that," says Jan. "Forget her."

Tilly pauses, and he thinks she too is dreaming a name, but when she speaks it is to say: "Do you forget her? Have you forgotten Mercy?"

"No." It is the truth. Should he say otherwise?

Tilly fixes him with still, dark eyes, but her words are headlong: "Did you love her? Do you love her?"

This is more complicated. As he frames his answer, he sees his pausing is making her fearful, and he wants so much for her not to be fearful. "I loved her," he says, and watches Tilly jerk, stiffen, "as you loved her. Because you did love her once, didn't you? You were friends. You saw something in her? Wanted it for yourself?"

Tilly's mouth is a line, but she nods. "Normality," she says.

"Yes," he replies, relieved. To look up at the night sky and sees stars, not grandfathers.

"Normal parents," says Tilly. "A mother, a father. An ordinary house, where they slept together. Ate together. A clean sofa. Quietness. No one ever shouted in that house, Jan. Ever. I loved being in that house. It didn't seem to have any secrets."

To hear the night wind and not the mumbo jumbo, that was what Mercy offered Jan. She held out the promise that the stars wouldn't clamour in his ears. But having the stars clamour in his ears is all that Jan knows, all he understands.

"And also she liked me," Tilly says. "Mercy liked me. Made me feel – not odd. More than this. Special."

"Yes," he says, "that is her gift." And he needn't tell Tilly about how his body jangled when Mercy was near, because it wasn't that, or not only that. Besides, if bodies were jigsaws, Tilly's is his fitting piece, his leg lying so very exactly against hers.

"Make-Believe," Tilly continues. "I deserved that. I called Mercy a liar. Because she saw. Saw my mother in a pool of vomit. And I wanted it not to be. It was me who lied. Lied about Mercy. Lied to myself. Tilly Make-Believe."

"Enough," says Jan. He puts his finger to Tilly's lips. "It's over."

"Is it?"

"Walk forward, Tilly Weaver."

"Tilly M. Weaver," she says.

"Tilly... Mountain Weaver," he replies.

"Mountain!" she exclaims.

"Yes. Tilly Mountain Weaver, Tilly Music Weaver, Tilly... Metamorphosis, Tilly Mourning and Moving-On. Tilly Mystery and Magic. Tilly Mine. Mine?" His finger has moved, to cup her chin.

"Tilly yours?" She gives it back to him as a question. As though she cannot admit to his wanting her. And maybe he hasn't made it clear, because he too is afraid. But she hasn't moved his hand.

"Tilly Mine," he says and draws her nearer still.

"Tilly Moondrop?" she whispers.

And he nods, for there she is, a piece of the dark sky, broken off from the night, fallen to earth, bright in his arms.

48

I have good days and bad days. Sometimes I think Jan
is my prince and I am his Cinderella and we will both
live happily ever after. But I know that's just a story
and perhaps I've told too many stories. I'm good at
them, of course, but also frightened of them. I know
what they can do to you. I need to find some truth.
Jan says truth is fluid, he says you have to see with
your heart as well as your eyes. There was truth, he
says, in my red roses, my candles, my cinnamon
incense. And in Gerda. But I have to be careful because
I've been to a place where I lost track, where there
were so many lies, I could trust no one, especially not
myself.

Trust.

I still find that difficult. Some part of Gerda – which is some part of me – still whispers in my ear: "How could he love you? How could anyone love you?"

Jan says, how could he not love me when I contain mountains, oceans, rivers?

"And puddles," I say. "And stagnant ponds. And ice."

"Yes," he says, "of course."

And how, he adds, could he not love me when I have freed his tongue to speak? He reminds me how I accused him of having a problem talking. "And now," he says, "now!" He claims that I made it – make it – possible for him to say aloud things which previously he could only articulate inside his own head. And yet he is so often silent. For hours he can be silent. I can be sitting next to him and not know in which part of which universe he is in.

"Do you understand that?" I ask.

And he just smiles.

"Who is this boy?" My mother, returned from the detox unit asks. "Where does he come from? How do you know him?"

I don't answer this question because I can't. You see, it seems as though we've always known each other, some part of me recognises some part of him –

and vice versa. But isn't that just a story, the jigsaw, Yin-Yang story? It doesn't really happen, does it? Besides Jan could just walk away.

Then there's Mercy. I'm still afraid of her, of course; jealous, I suppose. How Jan looks at her – and he does. Though she no longer looks at him, has other fish to fry. Adam Silcocks. Adam won the Celeb Night music section, he played *Light My Fire*, and Mercy, apparently, spontaneously combusted. She won the Celebrity Lookalike Contest, of course, so the pair of them had to lead the dancing, his arm around her waist (no, I didn't see it, of course not, I was at Sanctuary Ward, but I've been told and I can imagine, that's my problem, imagination), the two of them twirling together in the spotlight. And is he gorgeous or what? I did overhear that, Mercy talking on her mobile phone: "You should see him. Adam Silcocks. Is he gorgeous or what? My perfect man."

Perfect. That's another thing. My perfect grandfather, Gerry. Has my grandmother told my mother about "perfect" Gerry yet? No, she has not. Grandma says my mother is still in a vulnerable state, only recently returned from hospital, she couldn't really cope with such information at the moment, it would be kinder to wait. I wonder how long Grandma will wait? She's already waited thirty years. Grandma's good at waiting. But it can't go on, I tell Jan, because otherwise I'll tell my mother: "Guess what? Your father wasn't a kind, loving, moral man after all. Your father was a shit."

Did it all start there? I sometimes wonder that. My mother growing up in the shadow of this perfect dead man, whose gap she could never fill. So whatever she did, it could never be quite good enough, never quite make up the deficit. She was, by definition, inadequate. For Grandma's story was that Gerry loved her so much, that all other loves (my mother's for her mother, Grandma's for her) could only be pale shadows of that one great love. That one great lie. And then the iron hardening in my mother's soul as her own marriage failed, proving beyond all doubt that no one could love Big the way Gerry loved Grandma. Was this it? Or could all these things have happened to another woman and that woman have laughed her way to a bigger, happier life? Jan says this is not my story and I can't know the answers, and maybe I don't need to know them. But I do need to know. Because I'm afraid. I am, after all, my mother's daughter and I know what a little space it is between being tucked up warm in bed and reaching under Red Riding Hood's skirts for that hard little bottle of Vladivar.

"You are also," Jan says, "your father's daughter."

When he says this we both realise, with shock, how little we have thought of our fathers. "My father," Jan says, "was a white lawyer in Santiago." When he speaks of him, Jan always uses the past tense, as if he's dead. And who am I not to understand that? He does not know the man's name – was never told it and has never asked. Nor does he know whether the man had a long-standing affair with his Chilean maid, or just a hot one-night stand, or whether he raped her. The only detail he does know was that the man was married. It would probably be easier to find this nameless man in the city of Santiago than to find Violeta Veron, but Jan says he has no interest. The man does not exist for Jan.

"I have thought so much about my mother," Jan says, "but about him, nothing. I cannot explain why."

I leave the subject then. This is a pain I haven't known, and I have to respect Jan's quietness, his ability, for the moment, to let be. But of course I think of my own father and how I have grated against him all these years. He's a quick, volatile man, a tiny volcano always boiling just beneath the surface. And of course I've blamed him, thought that if he been only a little bit slower, more tolerant, even just kinder, then things might have been different. But maybe I'm just mouthing my mother's opinions. When I think of my father, I frame him so often in her words. *The trouble with you, Richard, is you always go off at the deep end.* I try to stand back, look at him afresh. It's not easy. My responses – her responses – are so ingrained. *Small body, small mind.* And simply: *I hate you.* But why would I hate him? I retreated into my stories, he retreated into his work. Was that so bad, so very different? *Oh, come on! He was a workaholic long before I was an alcoholic, can't you see the connection?*

Shush, Mama. Please shush.

I make this resolution at least. I will take more interest in my father. *Typical for it to be that way round.* I will be interested in what interests him, menus and the emptying of bins and problems with the laundry. I'll be patient, make suggestions. Wait until, perhaps, I see a glimmer of other things in him – and he in me. I will no longer lay my mother's anger at his feet, her resentment. And then we will see. *Oh, you'll see all right.*

Enough, Mama. Because you must have loved him once, so there must have been something to love. Besides, if I can be a stagnant pond and also an ocean maybe my father can be a roaring volcano and also a warm hearth.

Fat chance.

Be silent, Mama!

Why have I let her so dominate me? Why loved her so much, so blindly? I can't answer these questions, except perhaps to say that not loving her would have been even more frightening. Jan says maybe we should practise hating our mothers. Set a little time aside every day when we allow ourselves our loathing. I haven't got there yet. Of course I know, or rather I accept, that Mama can be weak, selfish, vindictive. But there is a difference between what the mind knows and the heart believes. Besides, she is still my Big.

When she came out of detox, I went with Grandma to fetch her. Grandma parked in the hospital car park. She didn't mention this fact and nor did I. But it felt like progress. As did the fact that we went up to the ward together. Marcia Wells, the staff nurse, was on duty; she gave me a leaflet, pressed it into my hand. It tells you all about something called "A Merry-Go-

Round named Denial". Even the title made me want to laugh. And cry. They've made up characters, like in a story. One's called the Enabler, the person who sees the alcoholic doesn't suffer from their drinking, rescues them like you would a drowning man. And I think back to that time when my father left and Grandma moved straight into our house. She did it, she said, to protect me, to give me some sort of security. But now I think maybe she did it to protect the old illusion, the one that our family was perfect, is perfect. But then, if Grandma hadn't cleared up the sick, I certainly would have done. So I'm an Enabler too. I too am to blame.

"You are not to blame," Jan says.

I'm afraid of losing Jan. I'm afraid of needing him so much I'll crush him.

"Don't be afraid," says Jan. "You can't lose me because you don't own me."

I think at first, in saying this, he is refusing me, pushing me away. But he says it holding me. And this is also something I have to learn, how to hold and also let free.

"Relax," he says, "Tilly Moondrop."

Moondrop! What a ridiculous name to choose. I

don't know why I said it that day. I feel so far from any such thing. The most insignificant setback can reduce me, make me crushed and small again.

"If I say it enough times," Jan says, "perhaps you'll believe it, grow into it. Your name after all. You chose it. What put it in your head?"

Just being with him that day, I suppose, feeling confident enough to risk, feeling he wouldn't laugh. And he didn't laugh, has never laughed at me. I hold on to that.

"Anyway," he says, "you are my perfect drop of moonlight."

"Don't say perfect."

"OK, my perfectly imperfect drop of moonlight."

"Are you laughing at me?"

"No."

Perhaps, to be really strong, I need him to be able to laugh at me and for it not to matter. But I can't think that far ahead. I have to take one day at a time. They say my mother is in recovery. I'm in recovery too. She goes to Alcoholics Anonymous and drinks spring water. I go to the bridge and drink Jan. He is the first person who has loved me who didn't need to, who wasn't supposed to. Then I worry that I've just substituted Jan for my mother, that I'm like some clingy little barnacle who just can't ever be by herself.

"So maybe you make a good barnacle."

"Are you laughing at me?"

"Perhaps."

So things do change, quietly, slowly. Jan comes to my house. Rings the front-door bell, walks in my hall, sits in my living room, eats in my kitchen. Grandma makes him food. My mother makes him food. My mother. She makes hash browns, without any fuss, as though it was an ordinary thing. We spend time in my room, listening to music, being silent together. Touching.

The house does not smell of vomit. It doesn't even smell of disinfectant. Though each time before Jan comes, I go about, sniffing. Polish, candlewax, dust, incense. I don't think it's the happy ending. It never has been before. My mother has always relapsed. But I'm trying to be grateful, to allow tomorrow to take care of itself.

When we go to the bridge (and we do go, Jan and I) I never think to run any more. I cannot imagine a single reason for running the bridge. I want to live. That too is a change.

Where we lit the fire beneath the elderflower, there is a blackened pile of ash.

"Something will grow," Jan says, "eventually."

So I always go to look. I feel there's something sacred about this piece of earth. A new beginning, a new hope. That, because of what happened here, this ground has the power to sanctify the past, bless the future. Yet it is six months before I see the first tiny push of green. I run.

"Jan, look!"

He comes to me, looks.

"It's a nettle," he says.

"A White Dead Nettle?" I hope.

He kneels down, observes the tiny jagged leaves. "No, a stinging nettle."

My face falls. Jan laughs.

"Tilly," he says, "even the stars are only so much gas and dust."

Blue Peter
BOOK OF THE YEAR

feather boy

NICKY SINGER

Catherine would say it all began in a time that is yesterday and tomorrow and eternally present. But then Catherine's a storyteller. I'm not a storyteller. I'm just the guy it happened to.

Robert is the class victim, the guy who's never picked for the team. So no one is more surprised than Robert himself when a strange old lady sends him on a quest to solve the mystery of derelict Chance House. Legend has it that a boy once fell to his death from an upper floor window. But what has this past to do with Robert's future?

To get to the truth, Robert must learn what it really means to fly.

Collins

An imprint of HarperCollinsPublishers

Praise for Nicky Singer's most recent book, *feather boy*:

"Cleverly and economically written, this witty, observant and moving book is a comic and contemporary drama about courage, love, memory and the power of stories."
Sunday Times

"*feather boy* is the most intelligent book for youngsters I've read for a very long time. Every 12-year-old will see a bit of themselves in Robert and won't be able to put this book down until *feather boy*'s emotional, thought-provoking climax. Fabulous."
Funday Times

"*feather boy* is more than just a story about Bullying. It's bigger than that. It's about finding your voice, shouting from the rooftops about something you believe in, refusing to back down, never giving up. It's enormously uplifting."
John McLay

"*feather boy* is simply fabulous... an emotionally intense suspense novel of the highest order."
Michael Thorn, Achuka

"If you only read one book this year, choose *feather boy*, for its memorable portraits of youth and age, its taut plot and, above all, its emotional ring of truth."
Jenny Morris, Lion & Unicorn bookshop

"Powerful and inspiring."
Financial Times

"A joy to read... A fascinating, emotional and captivating book that deserves wide recognition."
Sheila Wood, Books for Students

"Something unique and special."
Tara Stephenson, Waterstone's